HERO, TRAITOR, DAUGHTER

(OF CROWNS AND GLORY–BOOK 6)

MORGAN RICE

THE GIFT OF BATTLE

THE SURVIVAL TRILOGY
ARENA ONE (Book #1)
ARENA TWO (Book #2)
ARENA THREE (Book #3)

the Vampire Journals
turned (book #1)
loved (book #2)
betrayed (book #3)
destined (book #4)
desired (book #5)
betrothed (book #6)
vowed (book #7)
found (book #8)
resurrected (book #9)
craved (book #10)
fated (book #11)
obsessed (book #12)

CHAPTER ONE

Akila hung in the rigging of his ship and saw death approaching.

It terrified him. He'd never been one to believe in signs and omens, but there were some he couldn't ignore. Akila had been a fighting man most of his life in one form or another, yet still, he'd never seen a fleet like the one that approached now. It made the fleet the Empire had sent to Haylon look like a series of paper boats being floated across a pond by children.

It made what Akila had look like less than that.

"There's too many," one of the sailors near him in the rigging said.

Akila didn't reply, because right then he didn't have an answer. He'd have to think of one, though. One that didn't involve the leaden certainty that was crushing his chest. He was already running the things that needed to be done through his mind as he started to climb down. They would need to raise the harbor chain. They would need to get crews to catapults on the docks.

They needed to spread, because charging headlong into a fleet that size would be suicide. They needed to be the wolves hunting the great snow oxen, darting in, taking a bite here and there, wearing them down.

Akila smiled at that thought. He was almost planning as if they could win this. Who'd have taken *him* for an optimist?

"There's so many," one of the sailors said as he passed.

Akila heard the same words from others as he clambered back to the deck. By the time he reached the command deck again, there were a dozen rebels at least, all waiting for him with worried expressions.

"We can't fight them," one said.

"It would be like we weren't even there," another agreed.

"They'll kill us all. We have to run."

Akila could hear them. He could even understand what they wanted to do. Running made sense. Run while they still could. Form up their ships into a convoy line and go, running along the coast until they could break free and make it to Haylon.

A part of him even wanted to do it. Perhaps they would even be safe if they could get to Haylon. Felldust would see the forces they had, the defenses of their harbor, and would be wary of coming after them.

At least for a time.

"Friends," he called, loud enough that everyone on the ship would be able to hear it. "You can see the threat that waits for us, and yes, I can hear the men who want to run."

He spread his hands to quiet down the murmur that followed.

"I know. I hear you. I've sailed with you and you're not cowards. No man could say that you are."

But if they ran now, men *would* call them cowards. Akila knew that. They would blame the warriors of Haylon, in spite of all they'd done. He didn't want to say that, though. He didn't want to force his men to do this.

"I want to run as well. We've done our part. We've beaten the Empire. We've earned the right to go home, rather than stay here dying for other people's causes."

That much was obvious. They'd only come here after Thanos had begged, after all.

He shook his head. "But I won't. I won't run when that means abandoning the people depending on me. I won't run when we've been told what will happen to the people of Delos. I won't run, because who are *they* to tell me to run?"

He jabbed a finger at the advancing fleet, then turned it into the rudest gesture he could think of on the spur of the moment. That, at least, got his men laughing. Good, they needed all the laughs they could get right then.

"The truth is that evil is everyone's cause. A man tells me to kneel or die, then I punch him in the face!" That got them laughing harder. "And I don't do it because he's threatened me. I do it because the kind of man who tells people to kneel needs punching!"

That one got a cheer. It seemed that Akila had judged this right. He gestured to the spot where a scout ship sat, tied up alongside his flagship.

"Down there is one of us," Akila said. "They took him and his crew. They whipped him until the blood poured from him. They lashed him to the wheel and they put his eyes out."

Akila waited a moment to let the horror of that sink in.

"They did that because they thought it would scare us," Akila said. "They did that because they thought it would make us run faster. I say that if a man harms one of my brothers like that, it makes me want to cut him down for the dog he is!"

That got a cheer.

"I'll not order you, though," Akila said. "You want to go home... well, no one can say you haven't earned it. And when they come for you, maybe there will be someone left to help." He made himself shrug. "I'll be staying. If needs be, I'll stay alone. I'll stand on the docks, and their army can come to me one at a time to get cut down."

He looked around them then, staring at men he knew, at brothers from Haylon and freed slaves, conscripts turned freedom fighters and men who had probably started off as little more than cutthroats.

He knew that if he asked these men to fight with him, most of them would probably die. He was probably never going to see the waterfalls that plunged through the hills of Haylon again. He'd probably die not even knowing if what he did was enough to save Delos or not. A part of him wished then that he'd never met Thanos, or been dragged into this wider rebellion.

Even so, he drew himself up.

"Will I be alone, lads?" he asked. "Will I have to punch my way to the stoniest-headed fool among them by myself?"

The roar of "No!" echoed across the water. He hoped the enemy fleet heard it. He hoped they heard it, and he hoped they were terrified.

Gods knew he was.

"Well then, lads," Akila bellowed, "get to your oars. We've a battle to win!"

He saw them run to it then, and he couldn't have been more proud of them. He started to think, to give orders. There were messages to be sent back to the castle, defenses to be prepared.

Already, Akila could hear the sound of bells ringing out across the city in warning.

"You two, get the signal flags up! Scirrem, I want small boats and tar for fire ships at the harbor mouth! Am I talking to myself up here?"

"Quite possibly," the sailor called back. "They say madmen do. But I'll get it done."

"You realize that in a real army, you'd be flogged?" Akila shot back, but he smiled as he did it. This was the strange part of being on the cusp of battle. They were so close to possible death now, and it was the moment when Akila felt most alive.

"Now, Akila," the sailor said. "You know they'd never let the likes of us into a real army."

Akila laughed then, and not just because it was probably true. How many generals could say that they had not just the respect of their men, but true camaraderie? How many could ask their troops to throw themselves into danger, not from loyalty, or fear, or discipline, but because it was them doing the asking? Akila felt that he could be proud of that part at least.

As the sailor rushed off, he had more orders to give.

"Once we're clear, we'll need to put the harbor chain up," he said.

One of the young sailors near him looked worried by that. Akila could see the fear there in spite of his speeches. That was only normal.

"If we have the chain up, doesn't that mean we can't retreat into the harbor?" the boy asked.

Akila nodded. "Yes, but what good would it do, retreating to a city that's open to the sea? If we fail out there, do you think the city will be a safe place to hide?"

He could see the boy thinking about it, trying to work out where he would be safest, most probably. Either that, or wishing that he'd never signed up.

"You can go be one of those who helps put the chains up if you want," Akila offered. "Then head for the catapults. We'll need good people firing them."

The boy shook his head. "I'll stay. I won't run from them."

"Don't suppose you fancy taking over the fleet so *I* can run?" Akila asked.

That set the lad off laughing as he went about his duties, and laughter was always better than fear.

What else was there to do? There was always something else, always something to move to next. There were those who spoke about warfare being waiting, but Akila had found that waiting always contained a thousand smaller things. Preparation was the mother of success, and Akila wasn't going to lose for lack of effort.

"No," he muttered as he checked the lines of his flagship. "The part where they have five times as many ships will do that."

The only hope was to hit and move. Draw them onto the fire ships. Crush them against the chain. Use the speed of their own ships to pick off what they could. Even then, it might not be enough.

Akila had never seen a force this size. He doubted anyone had. The fleet sent to Haylon had been one designed for punishment and destruction. The rebel army had been a coming together of at least three great forces.

This was bigger. This wasn't so much an army as an entire country on the move. This was conquest, and more than conquest. Felldust had seen an opportunity, and now it was going to take everything that the Empire had.

Unless we stop them, Akila thought.

Maybe his fleet wouldn't be the ones to stop them. Maybe the best they could hope for would be to slow down and weaken the invading army, yet maybe that would be enough. If they could buy Ceres time, she might be able to find a way to win against what was left. Akila had seen her do more impressive things with those powers of hers.

Perhaps she would take on Felldust's entire army and save them the trouble.

Most likely, Akila would die here. If that could save Delos, would that be worth it? That wasn't the question. If it could save the people there, and the people of Haylon, would that? Yes, that was worth everything to Akila. Men like this didn't stop with what they had. They would descend on Haylon as soon as they were done here. If his sacrifice would keep the farmers of the island safe, Akila would make it a thousand times over.

He looked out over the water to where the fleet advanced, his voice softening.

"You owe me for this, Thanos," he said, just as the prince owed him for coming to Delos, and for not cutting him down on Haylon. Probably his life would have been a lot simpler if he'd done that.

Looking at the fleet ahead, Akila suspected it might have been longer, too.

"Right!" he yelled. "Get to your places, boys! We've a battle to win!"

CHAPTER TWO

Irrien sat at the prow of his flagship in a mixture of satisfaction and anticipation. Satisfaction because his fleet was advancing exactly as he'd ordered. Anticipation because of everything that would come next.

Around him, the fleet slid forward in near silence, as he'd ordered when they'd started to hug the coast. Silent as sharks coming after prey, silent as the moment after a man's death. Right then, Irrien was the glint of light on the point of a spear, the rest of his fleet following like its broad head.

His chair was not the dark stone one in which he sat in Felldust. Instead, it was a lighter framed thing, made from the bones of things he'd killed, the thigh bones of a dark-stalker forming the back, the finger bones of a man set in the arms. He'd covered it in the furs of animals he'd hunted. It was another lesson he had learned: In peace, a man should speak of his civility. In war, he should speak of his cruelty.

To that end, Irrien jerked on a chain connected to his chair. The other end held one of the so-called warriors of this rebellion, who had knelt rather than die in battle.

"We will arrive soon," he said.

"Y-yes, my lord," the man replied.

Irrien jerked the chain again. "Be silent unless commanded."

Irrien ignored the man as he started to beg forgiveness badly. Instead, he watched the path ahead, although he'd set the metal surface of his shield so he could watch behind for assassins.

A wise man always did both. The other stones of Felldust probably thought that Irrien was mad, leaving for this dustless land while they remained behind. They probably thought he couldn't see their plots and machinations.

Irrien's smile widened at the thought of their faces when they realized what was really happening. His pleasure continued as he turned to the coast, seeing the fires that were springing up there as his raiding parties landed. Ordinarily, Irrien hated the wastefulness of burned buildings, but for war, they were a useful weapon.

No, the real weapon was fear. Fire and silent menace were just ways to sharpen it. Fear was a weapon as powerful as slow poison, dangerous as a blade. Fear could make a strong man run or yield without a fight. Fear could make foes choose stupid options, charging in rash bravado, or cowering when they should strike. Fear made men slaves, holding them in place even when there were more of them.

Irrien was not so arrogant as to believe he could never feel fear, but his first battle had not brought it the way men talked about, nor his fiftieth. He had fought men on burning sands and on the cobbles of back alleys, and while there had been anger, excitement, even desperation, he had never found the fear that other men felt. It was part of what made it so easy to take what he wanted.

What he wanted now swung into view almost as if summoned by the thought, the endless strokes of the oars pulling the harbor of Delos into Irrien's view. He'd waited for this moment, but it wasn't the one he'd dreamed of. That would only come once this was done, and he'd taken all that was worth taking.

The city was a low and stinking thing, in spite of its fame, like all the cities of men. It didn't have the grandeur of the endless dust, or the stark beauty of things made by Ancient Ones. As with all cities, when you crammed enough people together, it brought out their true baseness, their cruelty and their ugliness. No amount of elegant stonework could disguise that.

Still, the Empire for which it formed a lynchpin was a prize worth taking. Irrien wondered briefly if his fellow stones had realized their mistake yet in not coming. That they occupied the stone chairs at all spoke of their ambition and their power, their cunning and their ability to navigate political games.

For all that, though, they'd still thought too small. They'd thought in terms of a glorified raid, when this could be so much more. A fleet this size wasn't here just to bring back gold and slave lines, although both would come. It was here to take, and hold, and settle. What was gold next to fertile land, free from endless dust? Why drag slaves back to a land blasted by the wars of the Ancient Ones, when you could take the land on which they stood as well? And who would be there to ensure he got the largest portion of this new land?

Why raid and leave when you could wipe away what was there and rule?

First, though, there were obstacles to overcome. A fleet stood in front of the city, if you could call it that. Irrien wondered if the scout ships they'd set loose had come back home yet. If they'd seen the things that awaited them. He might not feel the fear of battle, but he knew how to stoke it in weaker men.

He stood to get a better view, and so that those watching from the shore might see who ordered this. Only those with the sharpest eyes would make him out, but he wanted them to understand that this was *his* war, his fleet, and soon, his city.

His eyes made out the preparations that the defenders were starting to make. The small boats that would no doubt soon be aflame. The way the fleet was forming into groups, ready to harry them. The weapons on the docks, ready to target them as they came close.

"Your commander knows his business," Irrien said, dragging his latest captive to his feet by his chains. "Who is he?"

"Akila is the best general alive," the former sailor said, then caught Irrien's eye. "Forgive me, my lord."

Akila. Irrien had heard the name, and had heard more from Lucious. Akila, who had helped to free Haylon from the Empire, and held it against their fleet. Who, it was said, fought with all the cunning of a fox, striking and moving, hitting where foes least expected.

"I have always valued strong opponents," Irrien said. "A sword needs iron to sharpen it."

He took his sword from its black leather sheath as if to illustrate the point. The blade was blue-black with oil, the edge a razor's. It was the kind of thing that might have been a headsman's tool for another man, but he'd learned the balance of it, and built the strength to wield it well. He had other weapons: knives and strangling wires, a curved moon blade and a many-spiked sun dagger. But this was the one people knew. It had no name, but only because Irrien believed such things foolish.

He could see the fear on his new slave's face at the sight of it.

"In the old days, priests would offer up the life of a slave before battle, hoping to quench the thirst of death before it could settle on a general. Then, it came so that they offered the slave to the gods of war, in the hope that they would show favor to their side. *Kneel*."

Irrien saw the man do it reflexively, in spite of his terror. Perhaps because of it.

"Please," he begged.

Irrien kicked him, hard enough that the slave fell to his belly, his head sticking out over the bow of the ship. "I told you to be silent. Remain there, and be grateful that I have no truck with priests and their foolishness. If there are gods of death their thirst cannot be slaked. If there are those of war, their favor goes to the man with the most troops."

He turned back to the rest of his ship. He hefted his sword one-handed, and slaves who had been waiting for his instructions rushed to grab horns. As he nodded, the horns blared once. Irrien saw catapults and ballistae crank back, flames being set to their loads.

He stood, dark against the sunlight, his bronzed skin and dark clothes turning him into a patch of shadow before the city.

"I told you that we would come to Delos, and we have!" he called out. "I told you that we would take their city, and we will!"

He waited until the cheer that followed died down.

"I gave the scouts we sent back to them a message, and it is one I intend to fulfill!" This time, Irrien didn't wait. "Every man, woman, and child of the Empire is now a slave. Any you meet without a master's mark is there for you to catch and do with what you are strong enough to. Any who claims to have property is lying to you, and you may take it. Any who disobeys us is to be punished. Any who resists us is in rebellion, and will be treated without mercy!"

Mercy was another of those jokes that people liked to pretend was real, Irrien had found. Why would a man allow an enemy to live unless it gained him something? The dust taught simple lessons: If you were weak, you died. If you were strong, you took what you could from the world.

Now, Irrien intended to take everything.

The biggest part of this was how alive he felt right then. He'd fought his way up to become First Stone, only to realize there was nowhere left to go. He'd felt himself starting to stagnate in the politics of the city, playing out the petty squabbles of the other stones to amuse himself. This, though... this promised to be so much more.

"Ready yourselves!" he shouted to his men. "Obey my orders, and we will succeed. Fail, and you will be less than dust to me."

He stepped back over to the spot where the former sailor still lay, his head extended beyond the edge of the ship. He probably thought that was the extent of it. Irrien had found that they hoped things would get no worse, instead of seeing the danger and acting.

"You could have died fighting," he said, his great sword still lifted. "You could have died a man, rather than a pitiful sacrifice."

The man turned, staring up at him. "You said... you said that you didn't believe in that."

Irrien shrugged. "Priests are fools, but people believe their foolishness. If it will inspire them to fight harder, who am I to object?"

He pinned the slave in place with one boot, making sure that all those there could see it. He wanted everyone to see the moment when his conquest began.

"I give you to death," he called out. "You, and all who stand against us!"

He brought his sword down, stabbing into the pitiful scum's chest, spearing the heart. Irrien didn't wait. He lifted it again, and for once, his headsman's blade performed its original duty. It cleaved through the enslaved sailor's neck cleanly. Not mercy, but pride, because the First Stone would never keep a weapon with less than a perfect edge.

He lifted the blade with the edge still bloody.

"Begin!"

Horns sounded, the sky filled with fire as the catapults launched and archers shot arrows out toward their foes. Smaller ships snaked out toward their targets.

For a moment, Irrien found himself thinking of this "Akila," the man who had to be standing there waiting for what was to come. He wondered if his would-be foe was afraid right then.

He should be.

CHAPTER THREE

Thanos knelt over the body of his brother, and for a moment or two it felt as though the world had stopped. He didn't know what to think or feel in that moment. He didn't know what to do next.

He'd been expecting some sense of triumph when he finally killed Lucious, or at least some sense of relief that it was finally all over. He'd been expecting to finally feel that the people he cared about were safe.

Instead, Thanos found grief welling up inside him, tears falling for a brother who had probably never deserved them. But that didn't matter now. What mattered was that Lucious *was* his half-brother, and he was gone.

He was dead, with Thanos's dagger in his heart. Thanos could feel Lucious's blood on his hands, and there seemed like so much of it to hold in one body. Some small part of him expected there to be something different about it all, for there to be some sign there of the madness that had gripped Lucious, or the grasping evil that had seemed to fill him. Instead, Lucious was just a silent, empty shell.

Thanos wanted to do something then for his brother; to see him buried, or hand him to a priest at least. Even as he thought of it, though, he knew that he couldn't. His brother's own words meant that it was impossible.

Felldust was invading the Empire, and if Thanos wanted to be able to do anything to help the people he cared about, he had to go *now*.

He stood, collecting his sword, ready to race for the door. He took Lucious's as well. Of all the things his brother had held close, the tools of violence had seemed like the closest. Thanos stood there with them both in his hands, surprised to find how well they matched. He was almost as surprised to find a collection of the inn's patrons blocking his way.

"He said you were Prince Thanos," a bushy-bearded man said, fingering the edge of a knife. "That true?"

"The stones will pay good money for a captive like you," another said.

A third nodded. "And if they don't, the slavers will."

They started forward, and Thanos didn't wait. Instead, he charged. His shoulder slammed into the nearest, knocking him back into a table. Thanos was already lashing out, cutting at the arm of the knifeman.

Thanos heard him cry out as the blade bit into his forearm, but he was already moving, kicking the third man back into a spot where four men hadn't stopped playing dice, even for the battle he'd just had with Lucious. One of them snarled and turned then, grabbing at the thug.

In moments, the inn managed to do what it hadn't when Lucious had been the one fighting: it erupted into a full-scale brawl. Men who had been content to stand by while Thanos and his brother traded sword blows now threw punches and drew knives. One grabbed for a chair, swinging it at Thanos's head. Thanos sidestepped, hacking a lump from the wood as he redirected the swing into yet another of the patrons.

He could have stayed to fight, but the thought of the danger Ceres might be in pushed him into a run. He'd been so sure that he could stop the invasion if he only got to Lucious, and then there would be enough time to find the truth about his parentage, discover the proof he needed, and make his way back to Delos. Now, there was no time for any of it.

Thanos sprinted for the door. He dropped and skidded under the grabbing hands of a man who tried to stop him, scraping a shallow cut across his thigh. He ran out into the streets there…

…straight into some of the worst dust Thanos had seen since he'd come to the city. He didn't slow. He just jammed his twin blades into his belt, pulled up his scarf against the dust, and pushed forward as best he could.

Behind him, Thanos could hear the sounds of men trying to follow, although how they hoped to see him well enough to catch up in this weather, he didn't know. Thanos groped his way along like a blind man, passing a merchant who was packing away his cart, then a pair of soldiers who were cursing as they huddled in a doorway against the dust.

"Look at that madman!" Thanos heard one of them call in Felldust's tongue.

"Probably hurrying to join the invasion. I hear Fourth Stone Vexa has started to send more of a fleet, while the other three are still plotting. The First Stone has stolen a march on them."

"Always does," the first replied.

Thanos was away into the dust by then though, seeking his route by the vague shapes of the buildings, watching out for the signs that hung above the streets, lit by oil lamps. There were stone carvings too, obviously intended so that the locals could find their way from the street of the carved bear to that of the knotted snakes by touch if they needed.

Thanos didn't know enough about the system to be able to use it, but even so, he pressed on through the dust.

There were others doing the same, and several times, Thanos stopped, trying to make out whether the booted feet he heard were those of pursuers or not. Once, he pressed in behind the curved iron bulk of a windbreak, his swords finding his way into his hands, certain that those following from the inn had caught up.

Instead, a team of slaves raced by, faces wrapped against the dust, carrying a palanquin from within which Thanos could hear a merchant urging them on.

"Faster, you curs! Faster, or I'll have you impaled. We need to get to the harbor before we miss the spoils."

Thanos watched them, tracking along behind the palanquin on the basis that those carrying it probably knew the way better than he did. He couldn't track it too closely, because in a city like Port Leeward, everyone kept a watch for would-be robbers or killers, but even so, he managed to follow it along the length of several streets before it disappeared into the dust.

Thanos stood there for a second or two, catching his breath, and as quickly as it had come, the dust storm lifted, giving him a view out over the harbor.

What he saw there made Thanos stand and stare.

He'd thought that there were plenty of ships in the harbor before. Now, it seemed that the water was full to brimming with them, until it appeared that Thanos could have walked to the horizon on their decks.

Many of them were warships, but many more now were merchant craft or smaller vessels. With the main fleet already gone from Felldust, the harbor should have been empty, yet it seemed to Thanos that there wouldn't be enough room for another boat there. It seemed that everyone in Felldust had come there, ready to take their piece of what was to be gained in the Empire.

Thanos started to see the scale of it then, and what it meant. This wasn't just an army invading, but a whole country. They'd seen an opportunity to take lands they'd long been denied, and they were going to acquire them by force now.

Regardless of what it meant for those already there.

"Who are you?" a soldier asked, coming up to him. "What fleet, what captain?"

Thanos thought quickly. The truth would mean another fight, and now there wasn't the welcoming veil of the dust in which to hide. He had no doubt that he was as coated with it as any of the natives, but if anyone should guess who he was, or even just that he was from the Empire, this would not end well.

He briefly wondered what they did to spies in Felldust. Whatever it was, it wouldn't be pleasant.

"Whose fleet are you with?" the man demanded again, this time in a harsh voice.

"Fourth Stone Vexa's," Thanos shot back, making his voice equally harsh. He tried to inject the sense that he had no time for such interruptions. It wasn't hard to do right then, when he had so little time to get back to help Ceres. "Please tell me it's not true about her fleet leaving already."

The other man laughed in his face. "Looks like you're out of luck there. What, you thought you could sit around, saying farewell to your crew's favorite whore? You waste time, you waste your chance."

"Damn it!" Thanos said, trying to play his part. "They can't all be gone. What about other ships?"

That got another laugh. "You can ask if you want, but if you think there's not a crew that's full right now, you haven't been paying attention. Pickings like this, everyone wants a place. Half of them can barely fight. Tell you what, though, maybe I could find a place for you on one of Old Forkbeard's crews. The Third Stone is taking his time. I'd only ask half of any share you get."

"Maybe if I can't find the lads I'm supposed to be with," Thanos said. Every second he was there was a second in which he wasn't sailing back toward Delos with the one crew there who wouldn't try to kill him the moment they found out who he was.

He saw the other man shrug. "You'll not get a better offer this late."

"We'll see," Thanos said, and set off amongst the boats.

From the outside, it must have looked as though he was looking for one of the rare boats from the fleet he'd claimed, although Thanos hoped that he didn't find one. The last thing he wanted was to find himself pressed into service in Felldust's navy.

He'd do it, though, if he had to. If it meant getting back to Ceres, if it meant being able to help her, he'd risk it. He'd play the part of some Felldust warrior, eager to catch up. If it had been main fleet sitting there, he might even have made it his first choice, trying to get as close to the First Stone as possible in order to kill him.

Now, though, if he drifted along with this second fleet, he wouldn't get there until it was far too late. He certainly wouldn't be able to help. So he walked the planks between the many ships, watching warriors carry on barrels of fresh water and crates of food.

Thanos cut cracks in at least three casks, but no amount of petty sabotage would stop a fleet like this.

He kept looking, instead. He saw men and women honing weapons and chaining oar slaves into place. He saw dust-covered priests intoning prayers for good luck, sacrificing animals in ways that made the dust into blood-colored mud. He saw two groups of soldiers under different banners arguing over which of them got to go along a wharf first.

Thanos saw plenty that made him angry, and more that made him scared for Delos. There was only one thing he couldn't find among the chaos of the docks, and it was the one thing that he'd come there to find. There were hundreds of boats there, of every shape, size, and design. There were boats filled to the brim with tough-looking warriors, and boats that looked like little more than glorified pleasure barges, there to take people to see the invasion as much as participate in it.

What he couldn't see was the boat that had brought him there. He needed to get back to Ceres, and right then, Thanos didn't know how he was going to do it.

CHAPTER FOUR

Stephania ran through the castle, pushed on by the sound of the war horns, like a hart ahead of a hunting party. If she didn't get out now, there would be no escaping. She'd done enough when it came to Ceres.

"Let Felldust finish her off," Stephania said.

She retraced her steps through the castle, to the point where it connected with the tunnels beneath the city. She hoped that Elethe had kept her escape route open as Stephania had ordered. Now was a time to flee. If they were caught by the rebellion, that would be bad enough, but to be caught in the middle of a battle between it and Felldust's Five Stones would be far worse.

Except...

Stephania paused, looking out of a window toward the harbor. She could see the sky dark with missiles, ships on fire as a dark ribbon of invading vessels made its way closer. Stephania ran over to a spot where she could look out over the walls, and she could see fires beyond, too.

Whichever way she ran now, it seemed that there would be enemies. She couldn't just slip out over the water, the way she'd come into Delos. She couldn't risk slipping out into open countryside, because if it were her running the invasion, there would be raiding parties out to drive people back toward the city. She couldn't risk wandering Delos openly, because the rebellion's forces would try to snatch her.

Yet, where were those soldiers? Stephania had passed a few guards on the way in, her disguise more than enough to let her slip by them. There hadn't been many though. The castle had the feel of a ghost ship, abandoned in the face of more pressing matters. Looking out, Stephania could see rebels moving through the streets in bright armor and patchwork stuff. There would be a few figures close by, but how many, and where?

The idea came to Stephania slowly, more as a possibility than a reality. Yet, the more she thought about it, the more it seemed like her best option. She wasn't one to dive in without thinking. In the circles of nobility, that was a way to put yourself in someone else's power, or find yourself cast out, or worse.

There were times, though, when decisive action was the answer. When a prize was there to take, hanging back could lose it as surely as overeagerness.

Stephania made her way down to Elethe, who was looking back and forth between the tunnels and the city as though she expected a horde of enemies to arrive at any moment.

"Is it time to leave, my lady?" Elethe said. "Is Ceres dead?"

Stephania shook her head. "There has been a change of plan. Come with me."

To her handmaiden's credit, Elethe didn't hesitate. She walked along with Stephania in spite of the worries she must have had.

"Where are we going?" Elethe asked.

Stephania smiled. "To the dungeons. I've decided that you're handing me over to the rebellion."

That got a shocked look from her handmaiden, although it was nothing compared to the surprise there when Stephania explained more of her plan.

"Are you ready?" Stephania asked, as they got closer to the dungeons.

"Yes, my lady," Elethe said.

Stephania put her hands behind her back as if tied, then walked forward with what she hoped was a suitable show of fearful contrition. Elethe was doing a surprisingly good job of looking like a tough rebel with a freshly captured enemy.

There were a pair of guards near the main door, sitting behind a table with cards set out, showing how they were passing their time. Some things didn't change, regardless of who was in charge.

They looked up as Stephania approached, and Stephania was quite amused by the surprise she saw there.

"Is that... you've captured Lady Stephania?" one asked.

"How did you do it?" the other said. "Where did you find her?"

Stephania could hear the disbelief, but also the sense that they didn't know what to do next.

"She was creeping away from Ceres's rooms," Elethe answered smoothly. Her handmaiden was a good liar. "Can you... I need to tell someone, but I'm not sure who."

That was a good move. They both looked over at Elethe then, as they tried to decide what to do next. That was when Stephania brought out a needle with each of her hands, bringing it forward to strike the guards' necks. They spun, but the poison was a fast-acting one, and their hearts were already pumping it through their bodies. A breath or two later, and they collapsed.

"Fetch the keys," Stephania said, gesturing to one guard's belt.

Elethe did so, opening up the dungeons. They were full almost to bursting, as Stephania had suspected they might be. As she hoped, at least. There weren't any more guards, either. Apparently, all those with the ability to fight were on the walls.

There were men and women who were obviously soldiers and guards, torturers and simply loyal nobles. Stephania saw more than a few of her own handmaidens there, which struck her as a little foolish. The sensible move was not to insist on their loyalty, but to pretend to serve the new regime. The important thing was that they were there.

"Lady Stephania?" one said, as if she couldn't quite believe what she was seeing. As if she were their savior.

Stephania smiled at that. She liked the thought of people seeing her as their hero. They would probably do far more that way than simply from obedience, and she liked the idea of turning Ceres's weapons against her too.

"Listen to me," she said to them. "You've had a lot taken from you. You had so much, and those rebels, those *peasants*, dared to snatch it. I say it's time to snatch it back."

"You're here to get us out?" one former soldier asked.

"I'm here to do more than that," Stephania said. "We're going to take back the castle."

She hadn't expected cheers. She wasn't some romantic who needed fools to applaud her every decision. Still, the nervous muttering amongst them was a little grating.

"Are you afraid?" she demanded.

"There will be rebels up there!" a nobleman said. Stephania knew him. High Reeve Scarel had always been quick enough to challenge others to fights when he knew he could win.

"Not enough to hold this castle," Stephania said. "Not now. Every rebel who can be spared is out on the walls, trying to hold back the invasion."

"And what about the invasion?" a noblewoman demanded. She was little better than the man who had spoken. Stephania knew secrets about what she'd done before she married into wealth that would make most of the others there blush.

"Oh, I see," Stephania said. "You'd rather wait in a nice, safe dungeon for it all to be over. Well, what then? At best, you spend the rest of your lives in this stinking hole, if the rebels don't decide to kill you quietly once they realize how inconvenient prisoners are. If the others win… do you think being in a cell will protect you? You won't be nobles to them in here, just amusements. *Brief amusements*."

She paused to let that sink in. She needed them to feel like cowards for even considering it.

"Or we could go out there," Stephania said. "We take the castle and we close it against our enemies. We kill those who oppose us. I've already dealt with Ceres, so she won't be able to stop us. We hold this castle until the rebellion and the invaders kill one another, then we take Delos back."

"There are still guards," one said. "There are still combatlords here. We can't fight the combatlords and win."

Stephania gestured to Elethe, who started to open the locks on the cells. "There are ways. We'll gain more weapons with each guard we kill, and we all know where the armory is. Or you can stay here and rot. I'll close the doors and send a few torturers later. I don't care which."

They followed, as Stephania knew they would. It didn't matter whether they did it from fear, or pride, or even loyalty. What mattered was that they did it. They followed her up through the castle, and Stephania started to give orders, although she was careful to make it sound better than that, at least for now.

"Lord Hwel, would you mind taking some of the more able men and sealing the guard barracks?" Stephania said. "We don't want rebels getting out."

"And men loyal to the Empire?" the noble said.

"Can prove it by killing those other traitors," Stephania replied.

The noble hurried to meet her command. She sent one of her handmaidens to gather more, and asked a noblewoman to instruct those servants who would be obedient to Stephania's bidding.

Stephania looked around the group with her, judging who would be useful, who had secrets she could employ, whose weaknesses made them easy to control and whose made them dangerous. She sent the noble who had been so keen to avoid a fight to control the gates, and a cantankerous dowager to the kitchens where she could do no harm.

They gathered people as they went. Guards and servants came to them as they heard, their loyalties changing with the wind. Stephania's handmaidens knelt before her, then rose at a touch to be sent about their next tasks.

Occasionally, they found rebels who wouldn't submit, and those died. Some died in a quick rush of nobles, their weapons seized, their bodies broken as they were beaten to death. Others died with a knife taking them from behind, or a poisoned dart sliding into their flesh. Stephania's handmaidens had learned to be good at their tasks.

When she saw Queen Athena, Stephania found herself wondering which it should be.

"What is this?" the queen demanded. "What's going on here?"

Stephania ignored her bleating.

"Tia, I need you to find out how things are going at the armories. We need those weapons. I imagine High Reeve Scarel will have found a fight by now."

She kept walking in the direction of the great hall.

"Stephania," Queen Athena said. "I demand to know what's happening."

Stephania shrugged. "I have done what you should have. I freed these loyal people."

It was such a simple argument, and such a neat one, that it needed no more. Stephania had been the one to do the work of saving the nobles. *She* was the one they owed their freedom to, and perhaps their lives.

"*I* was locked up too," the queen shot back.

"Ah, of course. Had I known, I would have rescued you along with the other nobles. Now, excuse me. I have a castle to take."

Stephania strode off briskly, because the best way to win an argument was not to give one's opponent a chance to speak. She wasn't surprised when the others there continued to follow her.

Nearby, Stephania heard the sounds of a fight. Gesturing to those with her, she headed up a flight of stairs, searching for a balcony. She quickly found what she was looking for. Stephania knew the layout of the castle as well as anyone.

Below, she saw a fight that would probably have impressed most people. A dozen muscled men, no two of whose weapons or armor matched, were fighting in the courtyard before the main gate. They did so against at least twice as many guards, maybe three times as many before the battle started, all led by High Reeve Scarel. More than that, it seemed that they were winning. Stephania could see the bodies scattered across the cobbles in their imperial armor. The noble who loved to pick fights had picked one for the ages, it seemed.

"Foolish man," Stephania said.

Stephania watched for a moment, and if she had seen more of a point in the Stade, she would probably have found some kind of savage beauty in it all. As she watched, a man with a great axe slammed the haft into two men, then spun, catching one of them with the blade hard enough to nearly split him in two. A combatlord who fought with a chain leapt over a soldier, wrapping it around his neck.

It was a brave performance, and an impressive one. Perhaps if she'd thought, she could have bought a dozen combatlords sometime earlier and turned them into a suitably loyal bodyguard. The only difficulty would have been the lack of subtlety. Stephania winced as a spatter of blood managed to rise almost to the lip of the balcony.

"Aren't they magnificent?" one of the noblewomen said.

Stephania looked over at her with as much scorn as she could muster. "I think they're fools." She snapped her fingers in Elethe's direction. "Elethe, knives and bows. Now."

Her handmaiden nodded, and Stephania watched while she and some of the others there drew throwing weapons and darts. A few of the guards with them had short bows taken from the armory. One had a ship's crossbow, better fired braced on a deck than a balcony. They hesitated.

"Our people are down there," one of the noblemen said.

Stephania snatched a light bow from his hands. "And they were going to die anyway, fighting combatlords so poorly. At least this way, they give us a chance to win."

Winning was everything. Maybe one day, these others would understand that. Perhaps it was better if they didn't. Stephania didn't want to have to kill them.

For now, she drew the bow as best she could with her swollen belly. Firing down like this, it almost didn't matter that she could barely pull it back halfway. It certainly didn't matter that she took no time to aim. With the mass of those struggling there below, it was enough that she would hit *something*.

More than that, it was enough to serve as a signal.

Arrows rained down. Stephania saw one punch through the meat of a combatlord's arm, and he roared like a wounded animal before another three slammed into his chest. Knives flashed down to cut and skim, dig and gouge. Darts carried poison that probably had no time to act before the targets were punctured by arrows.

Stephania saw imperial soldiers fall along with the combatlords. High Reeve Scarel looked up at her with accusing eyes as he pawed at a crossbow bolt that had struck him through the stomach. Men continued to fall under the combatlords' blades, or found gaps in their defenses, only to find their moment of victory cut short by arrow fire.

Stephania didn't care. Only when the last combatlord fell did she raise a hand for the assault to cease.

"So many..." one of the noblewomen started, and Stephania rounded on her.

"Don't be so foolish. We have taken Ceres's support, and we have taken the castle. Nothing else matters."

"What *about* Ceres?" one of the guards there asked. "Is she dead?"

Stephania's eyes narrowed at that question, because it was the one thing about this plan that irritated her.

"Not yet."

They had to hold the castle until either the invasion was done or the rebels somehow found a way to beat it back. At that point, they might need Ceres as a bargaining chip, or even just a gift so that the Five Stones of Felldust could show their victory. Having her there might even draw in Thanos, letting Stephania have all her revenge at once.

For now, that meant that Ceres couldn't die, but she could still suffer.

And she would.

CHAPTER FIVE

Ceres was floating above islands of smooth stone and beauty so exquisite she almost wanted to cry. She recognized the work of the Ancient Ones, and instantly she found herself thinking of her mother.

Ceres saw her then, somewhere ahead of her, still robed in a mist. Ceres sprinted after her, and she saw her mother turn, but she still didn't seem to be gaining on her quickly enough.

There was a gap between them now, and Ceres leapt, holding out her hand. She saw her mother reaching out for her, and just for a moment, Ceres thought that Lycine would catch her. Their fingers brushed, and then Ceres was falling.

She fell into the midst of a battle, figures flailing about her. The dead were there, their deaths apparently not stopping them from fighting. Lord West fought beside Anka, Rexus beside a hundred men Ceres had killed in as many different fights. They were all around Ceres, fighting one another, fighting the world…

The Last Breath was there in front of her, the former combatlord as bleak and terrifying as he had ever been. Ceres found herself jumping over the bladed staff he wielded, reaching out to turn him to stone as she had before.

Nothing happened this time. The Last Breath knocked her sprawling, standing over her in triumph, and now he was Stephania, holding a bottle in place of a staff, the fumes still acrid in Ceres's nostrils.

Then she woke, and reality wasn't any better than her dreaming.

Ceres woke to the feel of rough stone. For a moment, she thought that maybe Stephania had left her on the floor of her room, or worse, that she might still be standing over her. Ceres spun, trying to come to her feet and continue the fight, only to realize that there was no room in which to do it.

Ceres had to force herself to breathe slowly, fighting down the panic that threatened to engulf her as she saw stone walls on every side. It was only when she looked up and saw a metal grille above her that she realized she was in a pit, not buried alive.

The pit was barely broad enough to sit in. There was certainly no way that she could lie full length. Ceres reached up, testing the bars of the grille above her, reaching down for the strength to bend or break them.

Nothing happened.

Now, Ceres felt the panic starting to rise. She tried reaching down for the power again, being gentle with it, remembering how her mother had corrected her after Ceres had burnt out her powers trying to take the city.

This felt the same in some ways, and yet different in so many more. Before, it had been as though the channels along which the power flowed had been burned through until they hurt too much to use, leaving Ceres hollowed out.

Now, it felt as though she was simply normal, although that felt like less than nothing compared to what she'd been only a little while ago. There was no doubting what had done this either: Stephania and her poison. Somewhere, somehow, she had found a method to strip Ceres of the powers her Ancient One blood gave her.

Ceres could feel the difference between this and what had happened before. That had been like flash blindness: too much too soon, fading slowly with the right care. This was more like having her eyes pecked out by crows.

She reached up for the bars again anyway, hoping that she was wrong. She strained, putting all the strength she could muster into trying to move them. They didn't give in the slightest, even when Ceres pulled at them so hard her palms bled against the metal.

She cried out in surprise as someone threw water down into the pit, leaving her soaked and huddled against the stone of the wall. When Stephania stepped into view, standing over the grate, Ceres tried to glare at her in defiance, but right then she was too cold and wet and weak to do much of anything.

"The poison worked then," Stephania said without preamble. "Well, it should. I paid enough for it."

Ceres saw her touch her belly then, but Stephania went on before Ceres could ask what she meant.

"How does it feel to have the only thing that made you special taken away?" Stephania asked.

Like having been able to fly, but now barely being able to crawl. But Ceres wasn't going to give her that satisfaction.

"Haven't we been here before, Stephania?" she demanded. "You know how it ends. With me escaping and giving you what you deserve."

Stephania dumped another bucket of water on her then, and Ceres leapt at the bars. She heard Stephania's laughter as she did it, and that just drove Ceres's anger. She didn't care if she had no powers right then. She still had a combatlord's training, and she still had everything she'd learned from the Forest People. She would strangle Stephania with her bare hands if need be.

"Look at you. Like the animal you are," Stephania said.

That was enough to slow Ceres a little, if only because she wouldn't let herself be anything Stephania wanted her to be.

"You should have killed me when you had the chance," Ceres said.

"I wanted to," Stephania replied, "but events don't always give us what we want. Just look at how things have gone with you and Thanos. Or me and Thanos. After all, I'm the one who's actually married to him, aren't I?"

Ceres had to put her hands against the stone of the walls to keep herself from leaping at Stephania again.

"I would have cut your throat if I hadn't heard the war horns," Stephania said. "And then it occurred to me that it would be an easy thing to take the castle back. So I did."

Ceres shook her head. She couldn't believe that.

"I freed the castle."

She'd done more than that. She'd filled it with rebels. She'd taken the people who were loyal to the Empire and she'd imprisoned them. The others, she'd given chances to, she'd…

"Ah, you're starting to see it now, aren't you?" Stephania said. "All those people who were so quick to thank you for their freedom turned back to me just as quickly. I'll have to watch them."

"You'll have to watch more than that," Ceres snapped back. "You think the rebellion's fighters will let you sit here playing queen? You think the combatlords will?"

"Ah," Stephania said, with an exaggerated show of embarrassment that made Ceres dread what was coming next. "I'm afraid I have some bad news about your combatlords. It turns out that the best of fighters still dies when you put an arrow in his heart."

She said that so casually, so tauntingly, yet if it was even half true it was enough to break Ceres's heart. She'd fought alongside the combatlords. She'd trained alongside them. They'd been her friends and her allies.

"You just enjoy being cruel," Ceres said.

To her surprise, she saw Stephania shake her head.

"Let me guess. You think I'm no better than that idiot, Lucious? A man who couldn't enjoy himself in the slightest unless someone else was screaming? You think I'm like that?"

It seemed like a fairly accurate description from where Ceres was standing. Especially given everything that was likely to happen next.

"Aren't you?" Ceres demanded. "Oh, I'm sorry, and there I was thinking that you'd put me in a stone pit, waiting to die."

"Waiting for torture, actually," Stephania said. "But that's just you. *You* deserve everything you get after all you tried to take from me. Thanos was mine."

Perhaps she really believed that. Perhaps she honestly felt that it was normal to try to murder your rivals in relationships and life.

"And the rest of it?" Ceres said. "Are you going to try to convince me that you're basically a nice person, Stephania? Because I'm pretty sure that ship sailed the moment you tried to send me to the Isle of Prisoners."

Perhaps she shouldn't have made fun of her like that, because Stephania hefted a third bucket of water. She appeared to consider it for a moment, shrugged, and dumped it over Ceres in a wash of freezing cold.

"I'm saying that nice doesn't come into it, you stupid peasant," she snapped as Ceres shivered. "We live in a world that will try to take all you have from you without asking. Particularly if you're a woman. There are always thugs like Lucious. There are always those who want to take and take."

"So we fight them," Ceres said. "We set people free! We protect them."

She heard Stephania laugh at that.

"You actually believe that foolishness works, don't you?" Stephania said. "You think that people are basically good, and all will be well if you just give them a chance."

She said it as though it were something to mock, rather than a good philosophy for a life.

"That is not life," Stephania continued. "Life is a war, fought any way you can find to fight it. You give no one power over you, and you take all the power you can, because that way you have the strength to crush them when they try to betray you."

"I'm not feeling very crushed," Ceres retorted. She wasn't going to let Stephania see how weak she felt in that moment, or how empty. She was going to create the pretense of strength, in the hope that she might find a way for reality to follow.

She saw Stephania shrug.

"You will. Your rebellion is currently fighting a battle with the army of Felldust. It might win, and then I will trade you for a path out of the city with all the wealth I can take. My guess, though, is that Felldust will wash through the city like a wave. I will let them break against the walls of this castle, until they are ready to talk."

"You think men like that will just talk to you?" Ceres demanded. "They'll kill you."

Ceres wasn't sure why she gave Stephania that much of a warning. The world would be a better place if someone killed her, even if it was the armies of Felldust.

"You think I haven't thought it through?" Stephania countered. "Felldust is fractious. It cannot afford to have its soldiers sitting, laying siege to a castle it cannot take. They would fight amongst themselves in weeks, if not before. They will have to talk."

"And you think they'll play fair with you?" Ceres asked.

Sometimes, she could barely believe the arrogance Stephania showed.

"I am not a fool," Stephania said. "I have one of my handmaidens preparing to play the part of me for the first meeting, so that if they try to betray us, I have time to flee the city through the tunnels. After that, I will present you, kneeling and in chains, to First Stone Irrien. An offering with which to begin peace negotiations. And who knows? Perhaps First Stone Irrien will find himself... amenable to joining our two nations together. I feel I could do a lot alongside someone like that."

Ceres shook her head at that thought. She would no more kneel on Stephania's command than on that of any other noble. "You think I'm going to give you the satisfaction—"

"I think that I don't have to wait for you to *give* anything," Stephania snapped back. "I can take anything I want from you, including your life. Remember that, in what follows: if it weren't for this war, I would have shown you mercy, and just killed you."

It sounded as though Stephania had as strange an idea about mercy as about everything else in the world.

"What happened to you?" Ceres asked her. "What made you into this?"

Stephania smiled at that. "I saw the world as it was. And now, I think, the world will see you as you are. I can't kill you, so I'll destroy the symbol you made yourself into. You're going to fight for me, Ceres. Again and again, without the strength that made people think you were so special. In between, we'll find ways to make it worse."

That didn't sound so different from anything Lucious or the royals had tried to do.

"You're not going to break me," Ceres promised her. "I'm not going to collapse and beg just for your entertainment, or your petty revenge, or whatever else you want to call it."

"You will," Stephania promised her in return. "You're going to kneel before the First Stone of Felldust and beg to be his slave. I'll make sure of it."

CHAPTER SIX

Felene had stolen plenty of boats in her time, and she was pleased to find this one was one of the better ones. It wasn't much more than a skiff, but it sailed beautifully, seeming to respond as quick as thought, feeling like an extension of herself.

"It would need more holes in it for that," Felene said, moving to bail out water that had washed over the side. Even doing that hurt, and as for the times when she had to row because the wind had dropped…

Felene winced just thinking about that.

She tested the wound gingerly, moving her arm in every direction to stretch the muscles of her back. There were some movements where it almost seemed as though she could ignore its presence, but there were others—

"Depths take you!" Felene swore as pain flashed through her, white hot.

The worst part was that every flash of pain brought with it memories of being stabbed. Of looking into Elethe's eyes while Stephania stabbed her from behind. Every physical pain brought with it the agony of betrayal as well. She'd dared to think…

"What," Felene demanded. "That you might finally end up happy? That you'd float off with a princess and some lovely girl, and the world would just leave you alone?"

It was stupid thinking. The world didn't offer the happy endings you got in singers' tales. Certainly not for a thief like her. No matter what happened, there would always be something else to steal, whether it was a jewel, or a slice of the map, or the heart of some girl who would then turn out to…

"Stop it," Felene told herself, but that was harder than it looked. Some wounds didn't just heal over.

Not that her physical one had, yet. She'd stitched it as best she could on the beach, but Felene was starting to worry about the puncture Stephania's knife had left in her back. She lifted her shirt high enough to douse it with sea water, gritting her teeth against the pain as she washed it clean.

Felene had been wounded before, and this felt like a bad one. She'd seen wounds like this among others, and generally it hadn't ended well. There had been that climbing guide who had found himself mauled by an ice leopard's claws when Felene had been trying to steal from one of the dead temples. There had been the slave girl Felene had rescued on a whim after her master had whipped her bloody, only to watch her waste and die. There had been that gambler who had insisted on staying at the table, even after he'd gashed his hand on a broken shard of glass.

The sensible thing to do right now, Felene knew, was to head back the way she had come, seek out a healer, and rest for as long as it took to get back to everything she had been. Of course, by that point, the invasion would probably be over, and everyone involved would be scattered to the wind, but Felene would be all right again, free to go off wherever she wanted.

It shouldn't make any difference to her how the invasion turned out, after all. She was a thief. There would always be things to steal, and there would always be those who wanted to hunt her down. There would probably even be more in the aftermath of a war, when things tended to get a little less tightly controlled, and there were always gaps for someone cunning enough to slip through.

She could go back to Felldust, rest up, and then find some fresh adventure to set out on. She could go off in search of long-lost islands, or head into the lands where ice closed over everything like a fist. There might be treasure and violence, women and drink. All the things that had tended to mix together so readily in her life to date.

What made her keep the small boat's tiller pointed toward Delos was simple: it was where Stephania and Elethe would be. Stephania had tricked her about Thanos. She'd used her to get to Felldust, and then she'd tried to kill her. More than that, she'd tried to kill Thanos, even if the rumors around Felldust suggested that he had at least survived through to the rebellion's capture of the city.

Felene found that she couldn't let what Stephania had done go. Felene had left plenty of enemies behind her when she sailed on, but she didn't like to leave unsettled debts. She'd fought a duel in Oakford once over an insult a year before, and once hunted down a locksmith who had tried to cut her out of her share, following him across half the Grasslands.

Stephania was going to die for what she'd done. As for Elethe…

In a lot of ways, that betrayal was worse. Stephania was a snake, and Felene had known it from the moment she set foot on the boat. Elethe had actually dared to make her feel something. For one of the first times in her life, Felene had dared to think beyond the next theft, and had started to dream.

"And what a dream," Felene said to herself. "Traveling the world, rescuing beautiful princesses and seducing fair maidens. Who do you think you are? Some kind of hero?"

It sounded more like the kind of thing Thanos might have done than something for the likes of her.

"My life would be so much easier if I hadn't met you, Prince Thanos," Felene said. She jerked on one of the lines for her boat, setting it skimming in a new direction.

She didn't mean it though. The main thing her life would have been if she hadn't met Thanos was shorter. She would have died on the Isle of Prisoners without him, and after that…

He was a man who seemed to have a cause. Who stood for something, even if it had taken Felene to remind him of what that was. He was a man who had been prepared to fight against everything he'd been brought up to be. He'd fought the Empire, even though it would have been easier for him not to do it. He'd been prepared to give his life to save the likes of Stephania, which was truly the kind of thing a hero did.

"I suppose if I had any sense, I'd be falling in love with you," Felene said as she thought about the prince. He was certainly a better person to fall for than the likes of Elethe. But you didn't get what you wanted in this life. You certainly didn't get to choose when it came to love.

It was enough that Thanos was a man to respect, even admire. It was enough that just thinking about the kind of thing he would do made Felene into a better person.

"If not necessarily a more sensible one."

Felene sighed. There was no point in all this trying to argue with herself. She knew what she was going to do.

She was going to Delos. She would find Thanos if by any stroke of luck he was still alive. She would find Stephania, she would find Elethe, and there would be blood for blood, death for death. Probably, Thanos would have argued for something kinder or more civilized, but there was only so far you could go in emulating people. Even princes.

Now, there was just the question of getting to Delos and getting inside. By the time she got there, Felene had no doubt that it would be a city at war, if it hadn't fallen outright. Felldust's fleet would probably be a floating barricade before the city, and it was a long established tactic in times of war to blockade ports.

Not that Felene cared about that kind of thing. She'd occasionally made quite a healthy profit from smuggling her way around blockades. Food, information, people who wanted to get out, it had all been the same.

Still, Felene couldn't imagine that Felldust's soldiers would be very welcoming to her if she were stupid enough to just charge for the city. Already, Felene could see fragments of Felldust's fleet ahead of her, vessels strung out across the water from Felldust to the Empire like jet beads on a necklace. The main fleet had long since sailed, but they were going in clusters now, forming groups of three or four, setting off together as they tried to make the most of the invasion to come.

In a lot of ways, they were probably the sensible ones. Felene had always had more of an affinity for the people who came up after a fight to steal than for the ones risking their lives. They were the ones who understood about looking out for themselves. They were Felene's people.

An idea came to her then, and Felene steered her skiff in the direction of one of the groups. With her better arm, she pulled out a knife.

"Hoy there!" she called in her best Felldust dialect.

A man appeared over the railings, holding a bow aimed at her. "Think we'll take all you—"

He gurgled as Felene threw the blade, cutting him off mid-sentence. He tumbled from the boat, hitting the water with a splash.

"He was one of my best men," a man's voice said.

Felene laughed. "I doubt that, or you wouldn't have made him the one to lean out and see if I was a threat. You the captain here?"

"I am," he called back.

That was good. Felene didn't have time to waste negotiating with those who weren't in a position to do it.

"You all off to Delos?" she demanded.

"Where else would we be going?" the captain called back. "You think we're out catching fish?"

Felene thought of some of the sharks that had hunted her on the way in to the shore. She thought of the body tumbling among them now. "Might be. There's bait in the water, and there are some big prizes in these parts."

"And some bigger ones in Delos," the voice called back. "You looking to join our convoy?"

Felene made herself shrug as if she couldn't care either way. "I figure an extra sword is good for you."

"And an extra fifty is good for you. But it looks as though you can fight. You don't slow us down, and you eat your own supplies. Fair enough?"

More than fair, since Felene had found her way into Delos. However careful the cordon around the city, Felldust's fleet wouldn't look twice at her when she was a part of it.

"Fair enough," she called back. "Just so long as you don't slow *me* down!"

"Eager for gold. I like that."

They could like what they wanted, so long as they left Felene be. Let them think that she was there for gold. The only thing that mattered was—

The coughing fit caught Felene by surprise, almost doubling her up with the force of it. It ripped through her, her lungs feeling as though they were on fire. She put a hand to her mouth, and it came away wet with blood.

"Are you all right down there?" the captain of the Felldust ship called, in a voice of clear suspicion. "Is that blood? You're not carrying some plague, are you?"

Felene had no doubt that he would make her travel alone if he thought she did. That, or fire her ship just to be certain that no disease got close.

"Got gut punched in a fight on the docks," she lied, wiping her hand on the railing. "It's no big deal."

"If you're coughing blood, it sounds bad enough," the captain called back. "You should go off and find a healer. Can't spend gold if you're dead."

It was probably good advice, but then, Felene had never been one to listen to such things. Especially not when she had better things to do. If it had been just gold on the line, she might have done exactly what the man suggested.

"So they say," Felene joked. "Me, I say they're not trying hard enough."

She let the other ship's captain laugh. She had better things to do.

It was time to kill Stephania and Elethe.

CHAPTER SEVEN

Every day, the convoy of former conscripts made its way around the countryside surrounding Delos, and every day, Sartes found himself staring at Leyana, trying to find a way to tell her how he felt having her around.

Every day, Sartes spent time trying to put it into words, thinking of the things someone more eloquent might have come up with. What would Thanos have said, or Akila, or… or anyone else who was half in love and didn't know what to do next?

He spent his time caught between thinking about Leyana and thinking of the things he ought to be doing. They went from village to village, passing out what supplies they had, giving back conscripts who had been taken from their homes, and reassuring people as best they could that the rebellion would not be another set of tyrants.

Every day, he tried to compose something to say, and every day, he found himself getting to the point of making camp without having done it.

"Are you all right?" Leyana asked with a smile. She'd taken to riding on the same wagon as Sartes, and Sartes had to admit that he liked that. When they made camp every night, her tent was never far away from his. Sartes liked that too. He found himself grateful that if they were to be attacked, he would be able to rush out and save her.

He found himself half hoping that someone would attack so that he could.

Was this what being in love felt like? Sartes didn't know. He didn't have enough experience with girls to know for sure, and it wasn't as though he could just ask someone, because he was supposed to be the leader, and he'd learned from watching Anka that leaders couldn't afford to be that uncertain in public. He had to be strong, so that they could keep doing what Ceres had sent him to do.

He wished that Anka were there to talk to, rather than dead. He wished that Ceres were there too. Maybe his big sister would have been able to give him some advice. Maybe she could have told him how she knew what she felt about Thanos.

They traveled down through a village, handing out food. As seemed to happen in almost every village now, people started to appear the moment it was clear that the conscripts weren't there to attack them. Far too many looked painfully thin, starving after Lucious had burned the countryside.

There were more of them now. Sartes had seen the lines of refugees, some carrying everything they owned. Twice now, his conscripts had come across thieves or bandits trying to rob them. Twice, Sartes and the others had driven them off.

He hoped it would be that simple with the invasion. Every group of refugees they passed brought rumors with them, talking about the great fleet that was coming, the battles that were raging on the open water around the city as Akila's fleet tried to slow the invasion.

A part of him wanted to rush back right then and help, but Sartes had to trust that his sister knew what she was doing. If Ceres had a role for him in the defense of the city, she would send a messenger. Until she did, the best thing Sartes could do was keep going, trying to make the countryside safer.

The next time they stopped, though, he took his sword from his belt, holding it up for everyone there to see.

"This is coming," he called out to the refugees. "You're running from it, but you won't be able to run forever. The invasion will spread beyond the city, so you might as well learn how to protect yourselves. Grab whatever weapons you can find. You're going to learn how to use them."

He hoped that he sounded enough like a leader for them to believe it. Plenty of them grabbed what they could: knives and hatchets, hoes, and even the occasional sword. Sartes tried to remember what he could of the lessons they'd forced into him in the army.

"You need to stand together if soldiers come," Sartes said, moving around the group of them. "You can't just look after yourself; you look after the people next to you as well. No, hold it lightly, or you won't be able to put the blade where you want. Stay in line. If you go off alone, you'll be surrounded by anyone who attacks."

To his surprise, he found Leyana at the end of the line, holding a knife as long as her forearm.

"I want to learn how to fight," she said. "The next time men come, I might not be able to hide."

"I won't let anything happen to you," Sartes promised.

She smiled at that. "That's sweet, but what if you aren't there?"

Sartes couldn't imagine not being there, because that would mean leaving Leyana's side.

"I'll be there," he promised. He realized what he was saying. "That is… I mean… if you want me to be."

"I want you to be," Leyana replied. "But if you're protecting me, it's only right that I should protect you, isn't it?"

That was a fair point, and Leyana seemed to get the basics of using the weapon quickly. Even so, Sartes hoped that she wouldn't have to fight anytime soon. He couldn't stand the thought of her potentially being hurt, and any fight came with risks.

To Sartes's surprise, when they left, a couple of men walked along with the wagons. Sartes frowned at that.

"They want to help fight the invasion," Leyana said beside him. "You said it yourself: we have to stand together."

"That wasn't what I meant," Sartes said.

Sometimes, though, it didn't matter what you were trying to do. It mattered what you did. Sartes just hoped that everything he did would prove to be enough.

***

They moved on, heading for the next village. There always seemed to be another village. When they finally stopped for the night, Sartes wandered from the road a little way. He spun at the sound of footsteps behind him, padding across the meadow grass, his hand already going to his sword.

He relaxed when he saw it was Leyana, although her presence brought nerves of a very different kind.

"I just wanted to see what you were doing, wandering off like that," Leyana said.

"I was just trying to get some time away from all the others," Sartes replied.

Leyana looked suddenly embarrassed. "I'm sorry, I could go."

Sartes realized what he'd just said, and how that had to sound. He didn't want Leyana thinking that he wasn't interested in her.

"No, don't go. I like having you here. I mean…"

"What do you mean?" Leyana asked. She gave him a look that Sartes couldn't decipher. "What is it you want, Sartes? Are we… do I mean something to you?"

"Yes, of course you do!" Sartes blurted, and then realized that he should probably be saying something more poetic. That was what people did, wasn't it? "You… you're like… the most beautiful… the…" He trailed off. "I'm sorry, I'm not very good at this."

She kissed him then. Sartes hadn't even dared to imagine what it might be like to kiss Leyana, because he'd been sure it wouldn't be possible. Yet when she put her arms around his neck and their lips met, it was better than anything he could have imagined. It felt as though his body was filled with fire and ice, both at the same time.

He kissed her back, not knowing if he was doing it right or not. All the things he'd been through since the rebellion started, but none of it had prepared him for this. He'd prepared for battles and sneaking around past enemies, not for kissing the most beautiful girl he'd ever met.

"I think," Leyana said when they pulled back from one another, "that you're better at this than you think."

"I just…" Sartes tried to get a grip on his stray thoughts. "It's just that there are all these things I want to say and do, and I want to tell you how I feel, but I try and I just get into a big jumble."

"Pretend that you're giving a speech to some of your men," Leyana said. "You do that well enough."

Sartes laughed at that.

"I'm not sure I'm ever going to give them a speech telling them how much I love them."

Again, it felt as though his mouth had run ahead of the rest of him.

"I'm sorry," he said. "I know it's far too early to say things like that, and I—"

"It's all right," Leyana said.

For a moment, Sartes thought that they might kiss again. Only the sound of someone else approaching made him turn from Leyana, and then it was reluctantly.

The man who was approaching was one Sartes didn't know well, but he was wearing the colors of one of the rebellion, and Sartes thought he recognized him from the forges. He was tall and lean, obviously out of breath, as if he'd just run to try to catch up. Sartes knew a messenger when he saw one.

He wasn't alone. It seemed that half the camp had come with him, eager to hear the news. Sartes did his best to hide his embarrassment. Whatever this was, it had to be important.

"What is it?" Sartes asked. "Did Ceres send you?"

There was something about his expression that said whatever it was he'd come for, it was serious. Maybe that was why so many of the others had followed him.

"Your father," the messenger said, still almost doubled up with the effort of it all. If he'd pushed himself that hard, it had to be important.

"Take your time," Sartes said. He offered the man a water skin.

"There isn't time," the messenger replied. "I've been looking for you for days, but I couldn't find where you'd be next. There's trouble. The invasion has come."

Sartes nodded. He'd heard that much.

"What does Ceres need?"

He saw the messenger shake his head.

"Ceres… has been taken. We went to the walls to fight the invasion, and the Empire took the castle back with Ceres in it. Stephania leads them, we think."

Stephania? That didn't make a lot of sense, but Sartes knew how bad that made things. Stephania had been the one to send him to the tar pits, after all. Stephania had been the one behind so much of this. If she was there, Ceres was in a lot of danger.

Sartes turned back to Leyana. "I have to—"

"You have to go help your sister," she said, reaching out to touch his arm. "I know."

The others stood around him then, as if waiting for orders.

"Tell us what you want us to do," a young man named Hedrin said. "Do we leave for the city now?"

Sartes looked around at the young men there. They were all conscripts, and far too many of him were his age, or even younger.

"I can't ask you all to do this," he said.

He saw Leyana smile at that. "I think you don't have to ask," she said. "This is for Ceres. More than that, this is for *you*."

"I still can't ask," Sartes said to the others. "I can't make you do this. I'm sorry, I need to get ready to go."

He didn't want to be the one responsible for bringing them back into a war. Even so, when he went to collect his things from around the campfire they'd been setting up, the others were there doing the same. It seemed that he wasn't going to stop them.

He saw Leyana gathering her things too, and ran over.

"You shouldn't come, at least," he said. "It will be dangerous."

"I don't mind dangerous," Leyana replied. "I *do* mind not being there next to you."

"Leyana—" Sartes began, but Leyana cut him off.

"We're doing this together," she said. "I'm going to help you, and together we're going to save your sister."

She made it sound so simple, yet there was so much they could all lose. Sartes swore then that he would keep her safe.

Whatever it took, he wasn't going to lose her.

CHAPTER EIGHT

Thanos hadn't thought that Port Leeward could get any darker or more dangerous, but somehow the cave ports managed it. He stepped into them, unable to shake the feeling that someone might try to cut his throat at any moment.

He kept his hand on the twin hilts of his and Lucious's swords, looking around for dangers. The trouble was that there were so many to find it was hard to pick one out from another.

The cave ports were cut into the cliff that overshadowed Port Leeward. Perhaps they had started life being eroded by the wash of the sea, but teams of slaves and engineers had obviously worked to enlarge them, creating a series of caverns like the froth on the edge of the tide. Shacks huddled up against the side, some stacked atop one another at improbable angles. There were jetties there, and merchants. Or smugglers. It was hard to tell the difference in a place like this.

"What's too evil even for Port Leeward?" Thanos asked himself as he made his way down there.

The difference was hard to spot at first, if only because Port Leeward already had spaces for its drug merchants and its slavers, its killers and its fences. There was an edge to this place, though, that said it was a shade or two darker even than that. Thanos spotted a team of men transporting a squirming sack onto a boat. He saw a crowd of hollow-eyed men, emaciated from years of chewing *traga* leaf.

He saw a man's corpse chained to a post, with a sign around his neck, the words "tax taker" scrawled in several languages. That said more about this place to Thanos than the rest of it put together. If Port Leeward was a place where Felldust took from the world, this was one where its inhabitants took what was left from one another.

When a man stepped toward him with a hungry look, Thanos half drew his sword. The figure slunk back toward the cave walls, leaving him be.

This was obviously a place for smugglers, but there were other boats there too. Thanos could see ships that were obviously out of Delos, the Southlands, and a dozen other places. He saw one loading grain, which didn't seem to fit with a place like this, and guessed that this had become the place for all those who weren't planning to join the invasion. Even with a fleet the size of the one heading to Delos, there had to be some ships still going to trade with other parts of the world.

That didn't make the cave ports any safer. If anything, Thanos guessed, it made them worse, putting the temptation of easy pickings in the way of some of the harshest people in Felldust.

He still couldn't find the ship he'd come to look for, but ahead, he could see the beginnings of a fight. A woman stood at the heart of a crowd of thugs, spinning a bladed chain to keep them at bay. Her soft, dark skin had been smeared with something like ash, lending it a grayish tint, while her head was shaved bald, revealing markings etched in cobalt blue. They matched the silk dress she wore, although that was stained with the dust of the city.

"Bone eater!" one of the thugs snarled.

"Cannibal whore!" another added. "We're going to make you beg to be killed. You and your coward people!"

If her appearance hadn't been enough, the insults sealed it. This was one of the Bone Folk of Felldust's farther coast. The stories about them were the kind of thing that sounded as though children had made them up to scare one another. Yet they were undeniably raiders, killers, and worse.

Even so, Thanos didn't like seeing half a dozen thugs threatening one woman. They seemed to be waiting for their moment. None seemed to want to be the first to move, but each seemed to understand that the moment that sharpened chain bit home, the others would be free to attack.

Thanos stepped into the ring of men, drawing both his swords.

"Time to step back, boys," he began, but then something blurred past his shoulder, and a man screamed as the chain cut into him. Thanos saw the woman charge past him, and suddenly he was in the middle of a fight.

Thanos saw the Bone Folk woman catch a knifeman's arm in the chain, wrenching and cutting, then kick out at another. He barely had time to register that, though, because two men were already charging at him.

Thanos ducked low, dodging the first attack, cutting with his right-hand sword to hamstring one of the attackers. He struck the other with the hilt of his other sword, catching him at the base of the skull and hearing the crunch as the man fell into unconsciousness.

He spun and saw the woman with her chain wrapped around another man's throat, while the last of the thugs ran.

"That's enough," Thanos said. "There's no need for—"

She dragged the chain tight, and the sharp edges all but decapitated her opponent.

"I decide what there is a need for," she said. She kicked the body into the water. "Fools. It is not worth carrying their spirits. Who are you?"

"I'm Thanos," he said. He could have given a false name, but he didn't plan to be here much longer. "And you?"

"Jeva," she said after a long moment. "You have my thanks. It would have been hard to kill six."

There was a grudging note to that, as though even admitting it cost her.

"Why were they attacking you?" Thanos asked.

He saw her spread her hands. "Why do outsiders do anything? They attack what they are too stupid to understand. My people will not bend the knee to join their war, and so they think they can kill me." She shook her head. "Now I must find a boat to take me home." She looked hopeful for a moment. "Do you have one?"

Thanos shook his head. "I can't find the boat I came in, and if I do, it will be going to Delos."

She shook her head again. "Fools. The world is full of them."

She walked away. Thanos let her, because in that moment he spotted a very familiar-looking ship.

He ran to it, as if worried that it might disappear if he didn't get there soon. Yet it was as solid when he reached it as it had been when he'd been traveling there. They seemed to be loading it for a voyage.

On the deck, Thanos saw the captain arguing with a figure dressed more like a pirate than a merchant, apparently in disagreement over the price of bales of a weed that gave off a bitter scent. As soon as the captain saw Thanos, he waved the other man away.

"Off with you. I've no time to waste with men who want to charge me so much. No, I mean it. Off my ship. It will be a lesson to the next man who wants to all but rob me."

The merchant looked shocked by that, but he still hurried off the boat. Almost as soon as he was gone, the captain rushed forward to enfold Thanos in a crushing hug. He stepped back and looked at Thanos with a serious expression.

"I see you're wearing two swords now, not one. It's done then?"

Thanos nodded. "It's done."

It seemed too brief a way to tell everything that had gone into killing Lucious, but maybe that was for the best.

"And how do you feel now?" the captain asked. "There are some things that leave their mark, and this is one, I think."

Thanos nodded. What he felt right then was more complicated than he could have believed. Satisfaction and justice, maybe, but also grief, and a sense that he'd failed even then. The invasion had still begun, and killing Lucious had done nothing to stop it.

"It needed to be done," he said, half hoping that he could convince himself of that.

The captain reached out to touch his arm. "It will get easier."

Thanos wasn't sure that he wanted it to, but he appreciated the sentiment.

"Where to now?" the captain asked.

That part, at least, was easy. "Delos."

"Delos? Are you mad?" The captain shook his head. "No. I will not do it. If I had known you would ask such a thing, I would have left while I could."

Thanos frowned slightly at that. "It was always the plan," he said. "I'd come, I'd… stop Lucious, and then we'd go home."

"That was before *home* turned into a place at war," the captain shot back. "We failed, Thanos. We were supposed to stop a war, but we couldn't. Now, to go back is suicide."

Thanos could understand that sentiment, but that didn't mean he could go along with it. Everyone he cared about was in Delos. *Ceres* was in Delos. He would find another way back if he needed to, but right then, he wasn't sure there was one. There was no way he could hide who he was long enough to sneak back with any other ship.

The captain could obviously see the determination in Thanos's expression, because he cut Thanos off before he could say anything more.

"No, Thanos. I mean this. You're trying to protect the people you care about, but I'm trying to protect my crew. It would take an army to be able to go to Delos, and I don't see anyone around here willing to stand up to Felldust's stones right now."

Thanos found his gaze drifting back over the dock, thinking about the things Jeva had said. About her people not wanting to bend their knees to the stones. He thought about the way she'd fought.

"What if I could find us an army?" Thanos asked.

"And where would you find one of those?" the captain asked.

Jeva was easy to pick out of the crowd. Thanos waved to her, and she only hesitated for a moment before running in the direction of the ship. She sprinted through the crowd with ease, dodging her way around the people in her way, never slowing.

The captain looked in the direction Thanos had gestured. Thanos saw the moment when he spotted the figure running toward them, because that was the moment his expression hardened.

"You want to bring a Bone Eater onto my ship?" he demanded.

"I want to do more than that," Thanos said. "You said it yourself, we need an army, and the Bone Folk have no love for Felldust."

That just added a note of exasperation to the captain's expression. Thanos felt the other man's hands clamp onto his shoulders.

"They have no love for anyone. They hunt ships and they steal. Do you know the things they do to captives? They'll kill and eat you so fast you'll wish you'd just picked a foreign shore for me to take you to."

Thanos appreciated the sentiment. There was even a part of him that wanted to go along with it. He'd been told by his father that there were answers about his parentage in Felldust. He could go off in search of the truth.

That would mean abandoning Ceres, though, and Thanos couldn't do that. Even if it meant taking the most desperate of risks.

"The Bone Folk will have their price," Thanos said. "If I can pay it, they'll be perfect mercenaries."

By now, Jeva was running up the gangplank.

"I guess I can drop you in a rowboat," the captain said. "But I'm not getting closer than that."

It would be enough. Thanos had to believe that it would be enough.

The captain gave Jeva a harsh look.

"Just don't blame me if you get yourself eaten."

CHAPTER NINE

When the torturers came, Ceres tried to fight. She flung herself at them, pulling together all the strength and fury she had. It made no difference. They grabbed her between them, and all Ceres could think was what it would be this time, and whether she would be able to keep from showing them how much it hurt her.

She had no way of knowing how long she'd been in the hole in the ground. Every so often they dragged her out to beat her, or chain her in positions that were agony to hold. They starved her too, feeding her only the tiniest bowls of foul-smelling food that made Ceres want to vomit at the thought of it.

Now, she guessed, they were planning something worse.

They dragged her to a vaulted space that Ceres recognized. It had been there for the training of the combatlords. She'd watched Thanos train there. She'd trained there herself. Now, though, the weapons were gone, and the dirt floor stood almost empty.

Almost, but not quite.

Poles stood in a circle, and on each one…

"No," Ceres said, horror flooding through her.

The skulls of the former combatlords sat atop the poles, in a bloody ring that seemed like a gruesome audience for whatever took place within it. How could anyone do this to men who had been her friends? To men who had done nothing but try to protect her?

"Do you like it?"

Ceres spun and saw Stephania entering the room with an entourage. There was a raised area above the dirt floor, from which owners might have watched their combatlords train. She took a chair there now, with servants and guards all standing around her.

"How could you do this?" Ceres demanded.

Stephania made a small gesture, and Ceres guessed what was coming, but she wasn't fast enough. Ceres stumbled forward as one of the torturers struck her across the back of the head.

"You will speak to me with the deference a peasant owes her betters," Stephania said. "You will remember that you are nothing, or you will be taught it. As for these men… you helped them to forget their place. I had no hatred for them until you got involved. Now, how does it feel to know you can't protect the people close to you?"

It felt to Ceres as though her heart were being torn from her chest, but she didn't say that. She wasn't going to give Stephania the satisfaction of seeing her broken like that.

"Still trying to be strong?" Stephania said. "The torturers tell me that it takes a lot to get a scream from you. But I'm not interested in your screams, so long as you break."

"You'll be waiting a long time," Ceres snapped back, and this time she did manage to duck the blow, half tripping the torturer who struck at her.

"Look at her," Stephania said, and this time, it didn't even sound as though she was talking to Ceres. Ceres guessed that she wasn't supposed to be important enough to speak to directly. "She puts so much of her pride in her ability to fight. Fighting is a useful tool, but it gets you nowhere alone. How much will it take out of her to be shown the truth, do you think?"

Ceres heard Stephania clap her hands, and saw three men in the colors of the Empire's guards step forward. They had no weapons, but that didn't make it better. It just told Ceres what might be coming. One by one, the guards dropped down into the training pit.

"Do you recognize any of these men?" Stephania asked. "Each of them hates you enough to volunteer for this. They fought you before, and you knocked them aside. You beat them like they were nothing. Apparently, it's the most humiliating thing that could happen. I plan to see if that's true."

"You'll need more than three," Ceres said, as the torturers stepped back from her.

"I doubt that," Stephania shot back. "As I told the men, you're not quite what you were, are you? You three, beat her but do not kill her."

She nodded and Ceres knew the moment for talking was done. Ceres slid into a fighting stance, trying to ignore the pain that came with every movement. She focused on the lessons she'd learned on the island of the Forest People. It didn't matter how difficult things had been there; the lessons had kept coming.

And Ceres had learned them. She leapt forward, striking at one man, then kicking out at the next. The blows slammed home, making them stumble. Ceres still understood the flow of combat.

The blows didn't knock them flying, though, and no flash of power came back to answer when the third man caught her with a stinging slap. It was so much of a surprise that for a moment, Ceres almost froze. She forced herself to keep moving, though. She spun away as one of the men tried to grab her, pushing him off balance, then turned to the next.

Another open-handed blow clipped her, and Ceres fought back, covering up and driving forward. At the last minute, she swerved around him and brought her knee up to catch him in the stomach.

Ceres spun away, stepping into a gap between the two others. She struck one underneath the ear, made a sound of pain as his foot found her thigh, and missed with an elbow that would have struck him in the temple otherwise.

The three men spread out, more cautious now. That was good. She was persuading them that she was still dangerous. She feinted toward one and then turned to another and grabbed his arm, twisting for a lock. She gave it up as the third came for her, catching him with the punch she'd really been aiming for.

Ceres smiled in satisfaction as she backed away again.

She was tiring, though, and even her best strikes weren't truly hurting these men. She needed to attack. She needed to be decisive, because she wasn't going to let herself lose simply because her powers weren't there to help her. She circled, trying to keep moving, determined not to stay in one spot long enough for them to grab.

One of the men stumbled and Ceres saw her opening. She knew she had to make it count. She lunged forward to kick the man in the throat, looking to end this, missed high and caught him on the jaw instead. He rocked back, but his hands went out automatically to wrap around her leg.

Another of the guards came in from the right to punch her in the stomach, hard enough to double her up. A slap caught Ceres from the side, making her reel. She tried to turn to fight back, but that just let the third man shove her off balance again.

Ceres lashed out blindly, feeling her foot hit home, but someone's foot slammed into the back of her knee and she went down. She tried to scramble back to her feet, but there were hands there holding her down, hitting and grabbing as they beat her.

As fast as that, what had been a fight turned into a beating. Ceres tried to break free from their grips, but there were three of them and they knew how to fight. She simply didn't have the strength left to break away.

They laughed as they did it.

"She's not so strong now, is she?" one laughed, slapping Ceres across the face.

"Weak little thing, really," another agreed, pinning Ceres's arms. "We could do anything we wanted with her."

Real terror rose in Ceres then as one of them tore at her tunic. Another started to tie her hands, stringing them out to tie them to one of the poles that held the combatlords' heads.

"No," she cried out. "Please, no."

She kicked out blindly, tried to scratch and bite and roll, but they held her, and they continued to beat her. When she managed to bite into one of the guards' ears as they came close to her, he stood, aiming a kick that would have doubled her up if they hadn't held her. They wrapped more of the ropes around her legs, tying them to more of the posts so that she could barely struggle at all.

Please, she begged her powers silently. *Please, if you're there, help.*

No answering flash of strength came, but to Ceres's surprise, salvation came from an unexpected direction.

"That's enough for now," Stephania called. Ceres had to crane her neck back just to be able to see her. "Leave her as she is."

Stephania was there then, above Ceres, with the serene expression of someone who knew they were perfectly safe. Ceres wondered how she must look to the other girl, who stood so pristine while Ceres was covered in the dirt of the training space, her clothes torn almost to nothing, blood smeared at the corner of her mouth. Ceres could even feel tears, although she fought to blink them away.

Stephania crouched beside her, brushing away some of those tears with her thumb in a gesture as humiliating as it was gentle.

"When you torment someone," she said softly, in what must have seemed like a comforting tone to those beyond, "going too far can be as bad as not going far enough. Push them too far, too soon, and there's no way to make it worse. I want you to think on that, Ceres. It will get worse."

"I… I'll kill you," Ceres said.

Stephania laughed, then slapped her. It was delicate in comparison to the slaps the men had already delivered, but that wasn't the point. The point was that Stephania was there above her, striking her, and there was nothing Ceres could do about it.

"No, you won't." She held out a hand, and one of the handmaidens near her passed her a knife.

Ceres could feel the sharpness of it as Stephania pressed it to her throat. Just a little more pressure, and it would open the veins there.

"Shall I do it?" Stephania asked. "Shall we all see what's so special about your blood?"

Ceres forced herself not to shrink back, although right then there was nothing she could do, regardless of what Stephania chose.

She saw Stephania smile. "As I said, you are more useful as a bargaining chip. Still, we can… improve things, can't we? There are always ways to make things… more difficult."

Ceres cried out as Stephania grabbed her hair, hard enough that Ceres thought she might rip it from her scalp. Stephania traced the knife slowly up her features, hovering over her eye so close that Ceres didn't even dare to breathe.

Then she hacked down at Ceres's hair like a butcher, again and again. There was no art or delicacy to it. Stephania probably had well-trained maids who did the most delicate of things with scissors to her own hair. This had nothing to do with that. It was simply a way of showing that she could do it.

She cut away Ceres's hair then, bit by bit, shearing her the way some farm hand might have sheared a sheep. Ceres cried at that, even though she forced herself to stay still. It wasn't just at the loss of her hair. It was at the helplessness that let Stephania do it. She held back the sobs only with difficulty. She had no doubt that Stephania could see the tears.

"Today, I wanted to show you how weak you are," Stephania said. "Tomorrow… maybe tomorrow I'll just want to hurt you. Either way, it won't be your choice, Ceres. I don't care if it's the rebellion or the stones of Felldust I give you to. I'll hand you to them broken."

She stalked away then, and her entourage went with her. They left Ceres. They just left her. She hauled at the ropes holding her and it made no difference. She struggled in the dirt and that just covered her in more of it.

Finally, she cried again. That didn't make any difference either. Her powers were gone, Stephania was going to keep playing her twisted game, and Ceres was too weak to stop her.

CHAPTER TEN

Stephania practically floated back from the pit on a tide of her own triumph. She'd enjoyed watching Ceres beaten the way she'd enjoyed few other things. It wasn't just watching her hurt; it was having the power to do it. Before, Ceres had been something untouchable thanks to the blood of the Ancient Ones.

Now, Stephania could prove to everyone who watched that she was more powerful. And it meant that she had a way to keep her followers distracted. That was important too.

Her mind flowed through all the possibilities there were for breaking Ceres, judging them one by one as she tried to balance what would prove entertaining with what would leave too many marks when the time came to give her away.

"I'll think of something," Stephania said, but Ceres couldn't occupy her thoughts completely. She snapped her fingers at Elethe, summoning her handmaiden forward. "Is everything in the castle as it should be?"

Her handmaiden bowed her head. "The guards who were suspect have been quietly purged, my lady. The last rebels have been driven out or captured. There was an attempt by a few to break in through the tunnels earlier, but it was repulsed."

Stephania nodded. She'd expected them to try something like that. She turned to one of the guards. "Keep watchers there, and set doors within the tunnels, strongly barred. An escape route is all very well, and we may need it if the negotiations do not go as planned, but a castle should keep people *out*."

"Yes, my lady."

Stephania turned to the next of those around her, and the next, taking in information, piecing things together from fragments the way a seamstress might have stitched scraps into a blanket.

"Is the girl prepared?" Stephania asked another of her handmaidens.

In answer, the woman brought forward a girl with golden hair, wearing a dress that had obviously been borrowed from one of Stephania's clothes chests. To someone who had never seen Stephania, she might have passed for her.

"No," Stephania said. "She's standing all wrong. If she stands as timidly as a mouse, First Stone Irrien will know who she is in a heartbeat. She must be convincing for the first meeting, until we can gauge their mood."

"I'll do better, my lady," the girl said in a trembling voice.

"And teach her to speak better," Stephania added to the handmaiden behind her. "If you can't improve on this soon, we may have to find someone else."

The handmaiden nodded, leading the girl away.

One of the guard captains gave her a report on the condition of the castle's walls, noting a couple of small gaps. It wouldn't have made any sense without a handmaiden's report on the noble who was trying to smuggle supplies out of the building. A spy told her about messages for the rebellion they'd taken along with the castle, and the figures in the rebellion that they'd managed to identify from them. Stephania filed that information away for later.

There were reports on the progress of the invasion, of course.

"The full fleet hasn't arrived?" Stephania asked.

"Some of it appears to have," one of her scouts said. "The rebellion's fleet seems to be harrying it as it advances, slowing some of it."

It was probably the only tactic the rebels knew, although given the size of Felldust's fleet, it was probably also the only thing that might work.

"Some of it?" Stephania asked.

Another of her handmaidens answered that one. "Parts of the fleet have landed beyond the city, spreading out to burn villages and besiege Delos. A few have made it in, and they seem to be fighting with the rebels in the streets."

It sounded like chaos, yet it could also be exactly the kind of plan the rebels might favor. Stephania knew better than to think that they were stupid. They knew about fighting against stronger opponents. They knew about traps, and ambushes, and picking off enemies piecemeal before melting away.

"What are the Felldust generals doing to deal with it?" Stephania asked. When no answer was forthcoming, she tried changing tack. "What are they doing with the areas they've moved into? The villages, the outskirts, all of it?"

There, at least, it seemed that some of her people had answers.

"They appear to be burning the villages," one of the soldiers there said. "Or they were. There are fewer fires now."

That wasn't necessarily a good thing. They'd obviously been using the fires to drive peasants toward the city. Now, it didn't mean they'd stopped attacking. It might just mean that they wanted the villages intact afterward.

"We were able to spot some slave lines from one of the districts where they've landed," one of her people said. "We tried to send a watcher to investigate."

"But you have heard nothing since," Stephania guessed. It was a foolish risk to take, but she didn't say that now. Instead, she found herself planning ahead, trying to work out the best way through what was to follow.

"We hold where we are," she said. "If imperial soldiers seek sanctuary here, contain them until someone can vouch for them. If anyone else tries to enter, *anyone* else, cut them down. We hold here, no matter what happens."

If they could do that, they would be able to force terms. They had enough supplies within the castle for a siege, and the potential for escape through the tunnels so long as they controlled them. Their walls would hold while Felldust took what it wanted from the city. They couldn't hope to run yet, or they would be hunted through the countryside. The better course was to wait. Let the invasion run out of momentum against their walls.

Then Stephania could start to put her proposals to First Stone Irrien. She would offer him Ceres as a gift to demonstrate his victory. She would offer gold from the treasury. Perhaps, if he was handsome enough, she would offer herself. After all, it was one thing to rule a castle, and still have an Empire to reclaim, but if she could seduce him, she could have two kingdoms at her fingertips.

But she would decide that later. In the meantime, the only real danger was discontent.

"Livinia? Arrange a masque, and see that all pleasures are provided."

"Yes, my lady."

Stephania led the way down to the throne room. The guards there raised their weapons in salute, yet what she saw within wasn't quite so welcome.

Queen Athena sat on the throne there, surrounded by a small coterie of nobles, guards, and servants standing in formal attendance. She looked up as Stephania entered.

"Stephania, did you not receive my command to attend me?" There was a hint of rebuke in the queen's tone. "I have been waiting here, and no one will tell me what is happening."

"Whereas I have been out in the castle," Stephania said. "Looking for myself."

That earned her a hard look from the queen.

"Careful, Stephania. Your role in taking back the castle has been noted, and I am grateful, but remember your place."

Stephania stepped forward. "I am more than aware of my place. Currently, you are sitting in it."

She enjoyed the look of surprise there. Stephania wasn't normally direct about these things, but there was something wonderful about the moments when she could be. They were the moments when something she'd planned had come to fruition. When she had power, and all that remained was to demonstrate its existence to others.

"Stephania," Athena snapped back. "You forget yourself! Kneel there before me, and I may forgive you when I am done speaking with the others here."

There was probably a point in her life when Stephania would have done it. When she would have sought the queen's favor above all other things. Well, things moved on, and Queen Athena had only ever been useful for the power she could provide to those who pleased her. Stephania had no time for those who clung on to such things longer than they needed through weakness, or some misplaced sense of loyalty.

"The others," Stephania said, looking at each of them in turn, silently assessing the nobles there and guessing which way they would jump. She looked beyond them, to the guards and the servants. "I wonder if you can even remember all their names, your majesty. I can. Their names, their secrets, the things that matter to them. I remembered enough to give them the titles they have sought for years, the gold you would never give them to help with their gambling debts." She looked to the nobles again. "You need to ask yourselves what is more likely to benefit you, serving a woman who knows nothing of you, or serving one who understands everything you desire and is prepared to give it."

"You dare?" Athena countered. She pointed to the spot in front of the throne. "I am the Queen of the Empire and you will kneel, or I will have you slain as a traitor!"

Stephania smiled at that. "You've never really understood power, have you, Athena? You think it's enough to yell that you are the queen, as if that gives you something. As if it is a tool, not a prize. You think people obey just because of the blood in your veins?"

"I think they will obey this," Athena snapped back, with a wave in Stephania's direction. "Take her! Hang her from the tallest point of the castle, for all to see!"

Stephania pushed down the knot of fear that came with those words. How could she not feel fear in a moment balanced like that? She'd made her preparations for this moment, having quiet conversations, making promises, occasionally reminding people of things that might come out if she died. If she'd misjudged it even a little, she would quickly find herself executed as a traitor. Only a fool would feel nothing in that moment.

Yet only a fool would show the slightest hint of it. Instead, Stephania stood at the center of the room, looking around at the guards there and the nobles. Not begging for their allegiance, but expecting it. One looked as though he might move toward her, but Stephania stilled him with a twitch of her hand. She filed his features away in her memory, in case she had to have him killed later.

For now, though, she returned her attention to Athena, smiling as gently as she could manage.

"It seems that your commands aren't worth much here," she said. "Shall we see how mine do? Kneel, Athena. Kneel, and I won't kill you outright."

Athena sat there for a moment or two, looking around as if hoping that this was all some dream. She rose as if she might try to defy Stephania even then. Then she crumpled like a storm-blown leaf, falling to her knees.

"There," she said. "Are you happy?"

"Yes," Stephania replied. "Very."

She stepped over to Athena, reaching down to touch her shoulder the way she might have reached down to a child.

"Power is wherever you find it," Stephania said. "It is wherever you can convince people it lies. Right now, it is in my hands."

"Compared to the army invading us, you have nothing," Athena said. "Felldust will wash through this city like a flood."

Stephania moved past her, standing in front of the throne, ready to sit. She took a heartbeat to savor the experience.

"Our former queen is right," she said. "The army invading us will go through the city. But we are not *in* the city. It is not a flood, but a rising tide. It will break against our walls and fall again, and then they will talk, because the five stones will want a clear victory rather than a muddy drifting away of their forces. We are safe here. You know me, and you know how clearly I plan these things. Do you think for one moment that I haven't accounted for what might come next?"

She could see some of those in the room starting to relax. This was part of the power she had now. They trusted that she was the one who might have a plan to save them. It tied them to her with threads of obligation as solid as steel. Still, they would need to be distracted from their questions. Stephania was glad of the entertainments she'd ordered. There was power to be found in being the only one thinking beyond their next wine glass.

Athena looked back at her with a venomous expression. Stephania's smile widened.

"You've never been good at disguising what you feel have you?" she asked. "You've never had to. Tell me, why should I keep an enemy near me?"

"You promised me," Athena shot back. "You promised you wouldn't kill me if I knelt. Look, all of you. This is the kind of oath breaker you serve!"

Stephania looked around to them. Athena had a point. Kill her directly, and the others would cease to trust her. Fail to kill her, though, and she would be leaving an enemy alive.

"You're right," Stephania said. "I gave my word. You will not be executed."

She gestured to two of the guards, who stepped forward without hesitation.

"Take Athena from here. Take her to the front gate of the castle and let her go."

Athena turned to her in obvious horror. "You're going to throw me out into the city? If the rebellion doesn't kill me, the invaders will. No, I won't leave!"

Stephania nodded to Elethe. "Find a bow. When the guards toss this idiot through the gate, count to a hundred. If she is still in range then, shoot her down."

"Yes, my... your majesty."

Stephania smiled at the correction. She lowered herself into the throne, enjoying the fit of it.

She could get used to being a queen.

CHAPTER ELEVEN

If Sartes had known how bad things were in Delos, he would have hurried back sooner. He drove his wagon up onto a rise in front of the city, and from there, he could see Felldust's warriors approaching it like some great swarm of insects ready to engulf it.

The naval battle beyond the city was raging in fire and bursts of violence, ships sweeping forward and then pulling back. Sartes didn't know how long it had been going, but for now at least, it seemed to be slowing the main bulk of the invasion.

It couldn't stop all of it, though. Sartes could see fires in the distance where villages had been burned, and lines of tents arranged in a rough crescent in front of the city. There were signs of violence inside the city too, with small figures running together in the streets, the distance rendering it silent in spite of the mayhem of it.

He could see other figures leaving the city, some of them fleeing in bunches, others sprinting alone. Sartes could see one group of figures in the dust-smeared armor of Felldust, bearing down on a group of those fleeing, their intent obvious.

"There," Sartes said, pointing. "With me!"

He cracked the reins, forcing the wagon forward. He turned to Leyana.

"Be ready to jump."

The wagon built speed as it thundered down the slope. Sartes steered it toward the fleeing figures and then past them, aiming for the armored warriors beyond. He saw their faces as the wagon bore down, and he forced himself to keep the wagon straight.

"Now!" he yelled to Leyana. "Jump!"

He wrapped his arms around her and leapt with her, making sure that he took the brunt of the impact as they rolled. Sartes came up just in time to see the wagon barrel into the ranks of Felldust's soldiers, crushing and scattering them.

He rolled to his feet, drawing his sword on instinct as some of the warriors of Felldust continued to rush forward. Some of them wore bright chainmail, but there wasn't the uniformity among them that there had been in the Empire's army.

That didn't matter, though, when they were charging toward him. Sartes braced himself for the attack, looking around at the peasants and townsfolk who'd been fleeing.

"Stand!" he yelled. "Stand and fight!"

They ran, though, and Sartes had to stand there while the might of Felldust's soldiers bore down on him. The first soldiers were almost on him when another wagon rushed past to slam into them, then another. He realized in a flash of shock that the other conscripts had started to copy his example. He'd hoped they might follow, but he'd never believed that they might do *this*.

Sartes watched the wagons strike home, and suddenly, it was Felldust's warriors who were running, fleeing back down the slope toward their lines. It should have seemed like a blessing, but instead, Sartes could only see the danger it represented; the chances of them returning in force.

"Are you all right?" he asked Leyana.

"I'm fine," she assured him with a smile. "We should keep moving, shouldn't we?"

They had to, but Sartes couldn't help staring after the crowd of people fleeing the city.

"They wouldn't help," he said. "We've done so much to help them, and they wouldn't help."

"They're just afraid," Leyana said.

It didn't seem to be enough of an answer to Sartes, but they kept going down toward the city anyway. There was a spot there that the rebellion had used as a smuggler's way through the walls. It was open now, and Sartes could see soldiers beyond it, fighting one another in a skirmish that rang with the sounds of steel and pain. When Sartes looked through the gap to see who was fighting, he hurried forward.

"Quick," he called. "We need to help them. My father's there!"

His father was swinging his smith's hammer with the strength of a much younger man while around him, rebels tried to push the warriors of Felldust back. His father had other smiths with him there, their hammers rising and falling as rhythmically as they might have when forging steel. They'd obviously been out working on the walls when the fight had come.

Sartes saw one fall to a thick bodied knife, cut down while trying to hold the invaders back. He plunged into the small battle, throwing himself at a warrior from behind and feeling his blade sink home. Another ran at him and Sartes barely ducked out of the way in time.

The others were there then, pouring in with him to attack the forces trying to get into the city from behind. At the same time, his father gave a shout, urging his men forward in a fresh attack.

There seemed to be blades everywhere in the next few seconds. Sartes ducked under the sweep of a sword, trying to stab back as it came at him and not knowing if he connected. He dodged past an attacker to make it to another who was grappling with Leyana. He pulled the man from her, tripping him, and the rest of the battle flowed over him.

It wasn't as brief as the fight to save the refugees had been. There, they'd had the crushing power of the runaway wagons. Now, it was down to violence and speed, but they still had the advantage of surprise. The invaders were expecting to be the ones descending with death and chaos. They didn't expect to be the ones being attacked.

Sartes saw his father sweep a man from his feet with his hammer, saw a pair of rebels diving on one of their opponents together, saw one of Lord West's men thrust right through an attacker.

Just as quickly as it had begun, it was done, and they stood panting as the adrenaline left them. Sartes looked around, and relief flooded him as he saw that Leyana was all right, and so was his father.

He rushed forward to draw his father into a hug. "I'm so glad you're safe," he said. "I got your message."

"Things are bad," his father said. "I'm trying to patch the holes in the walls, but they keep punching new ones, or finding them."

Sartes took Leyana's hand. "Father, this is Leyana. We met outside the city, and she's been traveling with us."

He wanted to say the rest of it: that he loved her. From his father's expression, though, it seemed that he didn't need to say it.

"I wish I could tell you to both run now and be happy," his father said. "But... we need all the help we can get to fight this invasion and free your sister."

Sartes nodded. He understood that, and the truth was that there was no way he would have agreed to go when Ceres was in danger. It seemed that not everyone felt that way though, because he saw a couple of Lord West's former men stand and head toward the hole in the wall.

"Where are you going?" Sartes demanded.

"Back to the North Coast. There's no winning this."

Anger flared in him. "You're going to desert? After you swore an oath to Ceres?"

One of the warriors climbed through the gap. The other shook his head ruefully.

"Ceres is gone," he said. "You think Stephania will keep her alive? Ceres is gone. The castle is gone. The city will follow soon. It's not as though most of the people here are standing up to fight."

"They're cowards like you," Sartes said. He felt his father's hand fall on his shoulder in a silent warning.

"I'm no coward," the warrior said. "I'll stand and fight, but I'll do it on the North Coast. I'll do it to protect my land and my people. This city is lost."

He ducked through the hole too, and Sartes wanted to rush forward to drag him back, but his father's hand prevented it.

"Let them go," he said. "We can't force people to fight, but *we* have to, and there isn't much time."

That part, at least, Sartes could understand. His sister was in the castle somewhere, in spite of what the men had said.

"We need to get into the castle if we're going to rescue Ceres," Leyana said.

Sartes saw his father smile.

"It seems you've found yourself a girl as brave as you are," he said. "Yes. Use the tunnels. I don't know if anyone will have closed them, but trying to find a way in through them is our only real chance. The walls are too strong to just scale. At least without Ceres and the combatlords."

He didn't sound that hopeful, but Sartes knew they had to try. The castle had always been secure, but the tunnels under the city ran almost everywhere. There had to be a way in, didn't there?

"If it's possible, I'll do it," Sartes promised.

"*We'll* do it," Leyana corrected him.

"And in the meantime, I'll hold onto the city," his father said. "I'll keep patching the walls, and we'll keep fighting the ones who do get in."

They'd decided then. The only difficulty now was doing it.

***

Sartes crept through the near dark of the tunnels beneath the city, holding up a smuggler's lamp to light the way while the others followed him. He kept the shutters on it low, illuminating only a short stretch of the path ahead. The others followed behind, forced to go single file because of the narrowness of the tunnels around them.

"Is this the right way?" Leyana asked, from close behind him.

"I don't know," Sartes admitted. "We used to think that there weren't any ways straight into the castle, or we'd have attacked it that way. Now... I know there were secret passages in the castle. I'm just hoping they connect, I guess."

Leyana reached out to squeeze his hand. "It's important to have hope."

58

The hardest part was that it was difficult to keep track of the direction they were moving in. Sartes was doing his best to map the turns and openings as they made their way along, but it was difficult to be certain. They could be heading in the wrong direction entirely, even though he'd spent plenty of time in the rebellion's sections of the old tunnels.

The one they were walking down started to open out, and Sartes saw the stonework around them change slightly, to more regular stone, dressed and decorated in a way that seemed familiar.

"I think this might be it," he said, although he kept his voice down so it wouldn't carry too far. "This way."

He led the way as the tunnel became a corridor, which gave way to dead, empty rooms that had obviously belonged to far older structures. There was even furniture in some of them, so old and rotted that when Sartes touched an ancient-looking chair, it collapsed.

The next room was circular, with sunlight visible far above. Fragments of mirrors set along the walls reflected that light, suggesting that it had once been some kind of well of light. For a moment, Sartes found himself dazzled just looking at it…

…and that was when the soldiers came.

They rushed from openings in the walls in a mass that caught their line of former conscripts unprepared. Sartes saw one slash his blade across the throat of a boy before he could even start to clear his weapon.

Sartes barely managed to bring his own to bear in time. He parried a stroke that would otherwise have gone straight through his heart, jumping back with no chance to counterattack. He parried again, swinging back blindly.

He knew he wasn't a great fighter. Not the way Ceres was, or Akila, or Thanos. When he'd succeeded before, it was always because he'd found ways to outthink his opponents, to surprise them or strike at them in unexpected ways.

Here, though, there was no room for movement, no time for planning. Sartes saw the Empire's men slam into the conscripts, and although they fought back, the slaughter in those first few seconds was horrible to watch. He saw swords sliding into flesh and out again, blood covering them. He saw conscripts struggling desperately, trying to overcome the surprise and fight back.

Sartes tried to fight. He thrust at one man, feeling his blade strike home, then barely managed to step back as a return thrust came at him. In an enclosed space like this, there was barely any room to dodge. Around him, he saw the former conscripts fighting bravely, their blades flashing in the light as they struggled with their attackers.

Sartes should have known. He should have guessed that Stephania would have the tunnels watched, and that the watchers would see them coming. He should have been more careful. He should have—

"Sartes!"

He spun at the sound of Leyana's voice. She was pressed up against a wall, a soldier holding her pinioned wrists with one hand while his other struggled with a length of rope. As if she were nothing more than another slave to be taken.

Fury flashed through Sartes then, and he ran at the other man. In the press of the violence, though, there was no room to do it. He found a soldier barging into him from one side. He pushed past and tripped as a leg hooked his ankle.

He briefly saw the world stretched out above him, with the figures of those fighting a little above, then the mirrored walls of the light well, then the open sky beyond. Sartes struggled to stand— and then something struck him on the side of the head.

He slipped into blackness, and even the sounds of battle faded to nothingness.

CHAPTER TWELVE

By the time Delos came into view, Felene felt as though she might keel over at any moment. Her back burned in a way that it shouldn't have, a long way from the dull ache that denoted healing.

"You should have stayed with the healers in Felldust," she told herself, but she didn't believe it. She had a task, and she was going to do it, whatever it took.

The small convoy she was traveling with was no help. Their captain had been serious about Felene only eating her own supplies, and even if there had been invitations to join the others on the deck of the adjoining ships, Felene wouldn't have trusted them. At the very least, she needed to maintain the illusion that she was one of them, and her Felldust accent wasn't good enough for a long conversation.

Seeing the battle that raged ahead, Felene found herself grateful that she *did* fit in. Felldust's fleet was like a stain on the water, held back only by the shore defenses and the harbor chains. Felene could see ships flying the colors of the rebellion trying to harry the edges of the fleet, fighting bravely, but she could see that their numbers were far too few to ever hold.

Then she caught sight of more.

There were half a dozen ships of varying sizes, including one great galley that looked far too much as though it had been stolen from the Empire. They descended on the convoy she was a part of the way raiders on land might have harassed an army's supply lines. It was a good tactic. If the fleet turned to help those joining it, then it would be distracted from its work while the attackers melted away. If it didn't, then it lost potential allies and supplies.

Which would be fine if Felene weren't on one of the ships they were targeting.

She broke away from the others while the squadron of ships bore down on them. She didn't try to break away completely though. The bigger ships of the rebellion had more sails and full banks of oars. All Felene had was a wound that continued to pain her and a need to get into the city.

She heard the moment when the great galley slammed into one of the ships she'd been tracking. It sounded like a tree falling as the ram on the prow tore through the side of the vessel. The rowers put it into reverse, while at the same time warriors near the front fought against those who tried to save themselves by jumping aboard the attacking ship.

There were battles going on all around Felene as the other ships closed and boarded the rest of the fleet. Battles on land were bad enough that Felene always tried to avoid them. Battles on the water were always more brutal, because there was no place to keep prisoners, and the monsters of the deep water were always circling, waiting for those who hit the water. Felene heard one man screaming as the sharks took him, then realized that she should be worrying about herself, because the great galley was turning in her direction.

Quickly, Felene started to unwind the mask that hid her face. Not that it would help. It wasn't as though anyone but Thanos knew who she was. That was her only hope. She pointed her small boat at the huge ship as if she might ram it, hoping that they wouldn't just pick her off with arrows.

"Thanos!" she yelled above the noise of the battle. "Thanos sent me!"

She kept yelling as she got closer, pulling just to the side of the galley where the oars rose to let her get close. Archers appeared at the side then. Felene didn't try to kill these; she just kept yelling.

"Prince Thanos sent me!"

Someone must have said something up on deck, because the arrows lowered and a boarding net dropped down the side of the galley. Felene understood what they wanted, but she wasn't going to let them dictate things so easily, so she took a grappling hook and lobbed it up there, ignoring the pain of the movement. She fixed it to her small boat so it wouldn't float away, then started to climb.

She soon wished she hadn't. Right then, every movement was agony. Halfway up, it felt as though she might collapse back into the water with the sharks. By the top, it was all she could do to pull herself over the railings and fall to her front on the deck. She looked up to see a wiry, tough-looking man watching her, recognized Akila, and forced herself at least to one knee.

"Consider yourself boarded," she managed between panting breaths. "I'd demand that you all surrender at once, but you might have to give me a minute."

That got a tight smile from the man there.

"I remember you," Akila said. "You're the one who brought Thanos to Haylon."

"And you're the one who said you weren't getting involved," Felene said. "I guess things change."

Akila looked at her for a long moment. "Do you need help? We have healers aboard."

He gestured, and a woman ran forward, examining Felene's back while they kept talking. Felene hissed in pain every time the woman touched her.

"Have you joined Felldust's army then?" Akila asked. "Should I be throwing you back over the side?"

"You might as well not bother, with the look of this wound," the healer said, prodding at the hole in Felene's back. It was all Felene could do to keep from spinning around and knocking her down.

"Please don't do that," Felene said. "It's bad enough I've been coughing blood half the way from Felldust, without you doing that."

"So you did come from Felldust?" Akila asked her.

They'd met before, but Felene had found that didn't always stop people from trying to kill you. Particularly if they thought you'd picked the wrong side. She decided it was probably a good moment for an explanation.

"Stephania fooled me," she said. "Thanos told me that he was going to try to save her, and when she came to my boat for an escape from Delos, I bought her lie that he was gone. I took her to Felldust, and she stabbed me in the back. Now I hear that she's returned to Delos."

"She has the castle," Akila said. "I've had messenger birds, but I can spare no men."

"Good thing I'm not one of your men, then," Felene pointed out. She forced herself to her feet in spite of the pain. "I'm going to find her, and I'm going to end this."

She didn't have to force that determination into her voice. It was there at the heart of her like the hard keel of a ship, holding it true and balanced. She was going to find Stephania. She was going to stop her, whatever it took.

"An admirable ambition," Akila said. "What makes you think you can do it?"

Felene gave him a hard look. "I'm not asking your permission."

She forced herself to stand straight then. She drew a blade, letting it shine in the sun.

"I've been across continents. I've stolen hearts and jewels and treasures you couldn't begin to imagine. I've fought my way past creatures and men. You really think one castle wall is going to stop me when I want revenge?"

She saw Akila smile at that.

"Probably not. Tell me, are you starting to wish that you'd never met Thanos?"

"Are you?" Felene countered.

She saw him shrug then.

"Sometimes, when we lose my men in one of the attacks. I'm throwing myself at their fleet, and I might as well be a blood-fly scraping at a horse's hide. I bite, and the tail swishes, and I have to fly again in case I'm squashed."

Felene understood that feeling. She was throwing herself at a castle singlehanded, after all.

"There are places I've seen where men run from the insect swarms," Felene pointed out. "Where they drain horses dry, or they die diseased afterwards."

"Not the most comforting of images," Akila replied.

Felene didn't care. She wasn't there to be comforting. She saw Akila's healer move to him, whispering something in his ear. Felene could tell from the general's expression that it wasn't good news.

"Your healer's telling you that I'm dying, isn't she?" Felene asked.

Akila hesitated for a moment, and then nodded. "Yes. I'm sorry."

Felene didn't have much time for sympathy then. By the sound of it, she didn't have much time for anything.

"Tell me something I don't know," Felene replied.

The healer didn't seem willing to stop, though.

"Your wound has festered," she said, "and worse, I think there is a flake of metal left in there. If I'd been able to get to it earlier, I might have been able to help, but as it is… I'm sorry."

She said that in the tones of someone who had already looked at too many dying soldiers today. Felene couldn't blame her for it. She had to save her blame for the people who deserved it.

"And you told Akila rather than me because you wanted him to decide if I ought to know. Because it might be better to send me off not knowing."

That got a slightly frightened look from the healer. Felene waved it away.

"I've known how this ends since I left," Felene said. "It doesn't matter, does it, Akila?"

She watched as he looked out toward the bulk of the Felldust fleet.

"No, I guess it doesn't."

He held out his hand to her and Felene took it. She could feel the strength there and the certainty. She hoped that she felt the same right then.

"Wish you'd stayed on Haylon when I gave you the chance?" he asked.

"Wish *you'd* stayed?" Felene countered.

He was going to die, as surely as she was. She might bleed to death, or die fever-ridden and raving. He was going to be crushed by the fleet. Either way, it was better than dying old and toothless years from now, their glory days long forgotten by all around them. Although somewhere in between those two points might have been nice.

"Be lucky," Akila said.

"I'd rather be deadly," Felene said. "Luck comes in two kinds, after all."

Akila nodded at that.

"We'll do what we can to help you," he promised, "but that's little enough."

"You've a battle to win, after all," Felene said. She made a joke of it, though it didn't seem like a funny one right then. "Maybe I'll climb onto their ships singlehanded and demand that they surrender."

Felene guessed she deserved that. Even so, looking at the fleet ahead, it did look pretty impenetrable.

"Can you do one thing for me?" she asked. "Can you give me a way in? There are plenty of spots where a smuggler might land, but I don't want to find myself chased by half of the battle while I do it."

"Then I'll try to move the battle for you," Akila said. Then he nodded. "I'll draw them off, give you an opening. But you'll need to be fast."

Felene was always that. Fast, and deadly, and certain. Soon enough, she decided as she started to climb back to her boat, Stephania would find out exactly how much of all three she could be.

CHAPTER THIRTEEN

Thanos stared at the space where Felldust's coast gave way to the villages of the Bone Folk, trying to hide the trepidation that he felt about going to a place like that. He'd heard as many of the stories about what they did to outsiders as anyone.

More than that, he still didn't know if this was the right move. His heart ached to be back in Delos, helping Ceres to defend the city. Yet he was just one man. Alone, he couldn't hope to stop the invasion. He needed allies.

"Are you sure about this?" the captain asked, as the crew started to lower the small boat that held Thanos and Jeva, the Bone Folk woman he'd saved on the docks.

"I'm sure it needs to be done," Thanos said.

He saw Jeva nod gravely.

"People must always do what is needful," she said. "And what the ancestors would approve of, of course."

"Which just happens to include butchering strangers," the captain called down.

Jeva gave him a contemptuous look, but Thanos thought he could see a flash of humor there beneath the pale ash that covered her face.

"Some of our ancestors were very violent," she said with a shrug. "Who are the living to dispute with the weight of the dead?"

Thanos felt the boat hit the water, and he started to row before he could change his mind. Over his shoulder, he could see the village advancing. Many of the buildings were wooden, but they'd obviously been dried out by the sun and worn by the wind, bleached until it looked as though Jeva's people lived in buildings made from bone. It didn't help that there was an arch down by the spot where the water met the shore, built from the bones of some sea creature so vast Thanos was glad he wasn't meeting it while it lived.

"I know that look," Jeva said. "It is the look all your kind get. It says that we are barbarians because we honor the dead properly and carry them with us. It is the look that comes before the insults, which come before the violence."

"Maybe I don't understand you," Thanos said, "but that's not the same thing as hating you."

"I have found it to be the same, many times," Jeva said. She shrugged again. "Your sailor was right. My people are not often friendly to strangers. This is a place for pirates, not farmers. After your assistance, I will help you to speak with them, but I can promise nothing."

That was already far more than Thanos could have hoped for.

They beached the rowing boat together, dragging it up to where the tide wouldn't claim it before they headed into the village. Jeva seemed to be leading him in the direction of one of the few stone built structures there: a many-sided hall with chimneys that belched out acrid smoke.

There were guards on the door, bare-chested and wearing kilts of tough leather, carrying staffs with bulbous ends, obviously meant for crushing. They frowned as Jeva approached, but she said something in a language Thanos didn't understand and they stepped back.

"What would have happened if I'd tried talking to them in Felldust's language?" Thanos asked.

"They would probably have ignored you," Jeva replied. "Barbarians are rarely worth speaking with. Remove your boots. The house of the dead must not be disturbed by the dirt of the living."

Thanos did it. He noted that she didn't ask him to leave his weapons.

Inside, it was obvious that this wasn't just a hall, but something close to a temple. People thronged about, talking and arguing, while above, on a raised platform, men and women in silk robes very similar to Jeva's stood in front of great fires that burned in pits.

Ordinary members of the Bone Folk came up to them, receiving something that they put on their tongues before returning to the crowd. Some paused to speak to those there in the language Jeva had used, and judging by the tone of the crowd those around them either called out their support or condemned their words.

"Is this some kind of religious ceremony?" Thanos asked. "Some kind of public forum? Something else?"

"All three," Jeva answered. "Those who go to the priests receive the ash of the dead to bind them to our ancestors. Some claim to speak with their voice, but that was a rare talent even in older days. Even the priests must cast runes and read signs. Most of those who speak say things that are their own."

Thanos saw one man step up to the stage, only for the priests to step back, shaking their heads. The man stood there firmly, holding out a hand.

A priest stepped forward and struck with a long dagger, slashing it across the man's throat. As he collapsed, the priest shoved his body into one of the fires, letting the flames consume him. It was so sudden and brutal that Thanos could only stand there in shock.

"Not all are judged worthy," Jeva said. "That one was a thief and a liar, who dared to sell one of our kind to slavers. He was told he could not be one with the dead anymore. They treated him as they would an outsider who demanded to speak when he should not."

"You're saying they'll kill me?" Thanos asked.

Jeva shrugged. "Maybe, maybe not. But you must take the ash if you wish them to listen. I will translate."

She led the way forward as if it were obvious that Thanos should follow. Maybe it was, because the facts hadn't changed. He needed the help of the people in this room. He stepped after her, following her through the crowd. It occurred to him as he followed that Jeva looked remarkably similar to the priests up there.

"Are you one of them?" he asked.

She looked back at him. "I have been through the rites, yes. They thought I might speak with the voice of the dead."

Thanos frowned at that. "Do you?"

She didn't answer, heading up to the platform. As Thanos followed, he saw people staring at him. Although they all seemed so strange here, he knew that he was the one who stood out as not belonging. When Jeva led him to the raised platform, Thanos even heard a few gasps.

He certainly heard the sharpness of the priest's tone when one of them stepped forward to speak with Jeva. She said something back, and Thanos had the impression of a fast, determined argument. Finally, Jeva stepped to a spot where an urn stood, taking a pinch of ash. Thanos thought she was about to consume it, but then he realized that she was holding it out to him.

"If you hesitate now," she said in a harsh whisper, "they will never listen to you."

Thanos opened his mouth, letting her place the ash on his tongue. It tasted bitter and dry in the moments before he made himself swallow.

"Speak to them in Felldust's tongue," Jeva said. "They will understand, and I will translate for those who don't."

Thanos nodded, looking out over the crowd of the Bone Folk. He'd addressed people before, but rarely with so much riding on the outcome, and rarely with such a terrifying audience.

"I'm here to ask for your help," Thanos said. "You know of the fleet that Felldust has sent against what's left of the Empire. They are attacking Delos as we speak. Without assistance, it will fall, and people I care about will die." He hesitated, just for a moment. "The person I care about most will die."

"All people die," a man called from the crowd. "And a war between the First Stone and some far-off city is no bad thing. It means that we do not have his ships harassing us. Why should we help you, outsider?"

Thanos had known that question would come ever since he'd come up with this plan. He'd been thinking about what to offer, and what to demand, ever since he invited Jeva onto the ship.

"I'm not asking you to do this from the goodness of your hearts," Thanos said. "The Empire has gold, and would be grateful to anyone who saved it."

He'd expected that to get a response. This was a community of pirates and robbers, after all. It was just a short step from that to being mercenaries.

"Irrien offered us your gold," one of those in the crowd called out. "He said we could keep what we took, but we didn't trust him. He has spent too much time attacking us."

Thanos looked out at the man. He had hair that had been spiked into elaborate shapes, and scars from plenty of conflicts.

"Then this is your chance to defeat him. If we do that together, he cannot be a threat to your people anymore."

"Or he destroys us completely for daring," the man shot back. "Anyway, the Empire has been no friend to us."

Probably because it didn't like having its ships attacked. Thanos could only think of one more thing to offer.

"What about land?" he asked. "You don't have much here. I am the son of a king, his rightful heir. I could give you new places to live."

"Away from the lands of our ancestors?" one demanded. "You would take us from our own lands?"

"That's not what I—" Thanos began but they were already shouting over him. Worse, one of the priests was advancing, the threat in his drawn weapon obvious.

Thanos felt Jeva's hand on his arm.

"Time to go, unless you want to end up on the pyre," she said.

Thanos didn't argue, although right then, it felt as though it didn't make much difference where he ended up. He'd been so certain he could get help for Delos, and he'd failed. He followed Jeva back out of the hall, but he kept looking back toward the platform as he did it.

"Who is this person who is going to die in Delos?" Jeva asked as they came out into the open air.

Thanos thought about not saying anything. It hurt too much to think about it right then. Yet he felt as though he owed Jeva something for getting him this far.

"Her name is Ceres," he said. "She… she's in charge of things there, I guess. She and I…"

How could he hope to explain everything between himself and Ceres to someone else? There had been too many things stacked one atop the other, between the rebellion, and Stephania, and thinking she was dead.

"Ceres?" Jeva asked. "The girl who has the Ancient Ones' blood running through her? This is for her?"

Thanos nodded. That seemed to be one detail that had spread rapidly.

He expected Jeva to take him back down to the small boat and send him on his way. Instead, she stood there, her hands balled into fists.

"What is it?" Thanos asked.

"The Ancient Ones… they are called that for a reason. They are some of the oldest of the ancestors. Those who claim to speak to the dead say their voices are loud even after all this time. Wait here. Do not move if you value your life."

She left Thanos standing there, heading back into the hall. He wanted to follow her then, more than anything, but her warning had been so clear, and so determined, that he didn't dare. Not for his own safety, but because this moment felt like a gossamer thread, and he didn't want to snap the possibilities embedded in it.

So he had to wait, instead, standing in the middle of the village, listening to the arguments coming from inside the hall and barely, *barely* beginning to hope.

When Jeva came out again, there was blood on the chain she carried. There was also a crowd of her people following her. They spread out around Thanos, looking at him now as though seeing him for the first time.

"What's going on?" Thanos barely dared to ask the question.

Jeva smiled grimly. "I told them that you spoke with the voice of the most ancient ancestors. They will not fight for you, but they will fight for one of that blood. You have your fleet."

CHAPTER FOURTEEN

Akila ran across the deck of his ship, shouting orders as he went and hoping that his men could keep up with them.

"Bear to starboard! Full stroke! Signal the others to regroup. They're getting too spread out!"

He felt the ship lurch as it changed course, its timbers creaking with the effort of coming about so rapidly. Speed was what it took, though, in the middle of the battle that had been raging in front of Delos. Speed was the only thing keeping him and his crew alive while they harried the larger fleet from Felldust.

When had he last slept properly? Akila had become good at snatching sleep when he'd been a rebel fighting in the mountains of Haylon. Now, there seemed to be a fresh attack looming every time he closed his eyes, dragging him up to assess and direct, command and hope.

With an enemy this powerful, sometimes hope was all there was.

Now, Akila ran his squadron of fighting ships at the edge of the enemy fleet's line, rushing past it with all the speed his rowers could pull from their banks of oars.

"Archers ready!" he bellowed, and the fighters waiting on the deck drew their bows. The great ballistae on the deck cranked back their strings, flaming bolts fitting into place. "Fire!"

They strafed the nearest ship as they passed, and Akila felt a flash of triumph as their flaming bolts caught the other ship's sails. But they didn't slow, keeping going while enemy ships near the ones they'd run by turned to follow. Akila let them. He could have ordered the rowers to find yet more speed, could have put up full sail. He could have sprinted for the open ocean. Instead, he let the galley jog there, its foes almost keeping up.

"Ready," Akila called out. "Wait for it... now!"

The oarsmen hauled, his pilot hauled on the tiller, and the galley turned. At the same time, more of the rebellion's ships came in from the side, catching the chasing foes between them right at the moment when they started to realize how far they were getting from the main fleet. The rebellion's ships closed, throwing grappling hooks, firing arrows, and charging across at their enemies.

The combat was quick and brutal. The battle for Haylon against the Empire had taught Akila the value of hitting fast, hitting hard, and not showing mercy to enemies who might be there to kill you tomorrow if you did. This was the same thing, carried out on the water, with strike after strike against their foes, designed less to win than simply to hurt them until they got tired of being hurt.

It wasn't working, though, and Akila knew he had to think of something else. The only question was what. Each strike hurt the Felldust fleet, but even the burning ships Akila left behind barely slowed them.

He stared out over the water, wondering if Felene had made it to shore yet. He'd given her the distraction he'd promised, but the rest would be up to her. He had to admire the kind of determination that would send her hunting across the sea for Stephania, in spite of wounds that would kill her. She was like an arrow sent after its target, no matter the consequences.

In that moment, Akila knew what he had to do.

"Form up the ships," he called out. "Signal the others. We're going to end this."

He set out his plans to his men. He could see the grim set of their features as he told them what he intended, but none argued. None even questioned. This was the best way. The only way.

He signaled, and they sprang into action.

At its start, it was a variation on the plan they'd used with the smaller groups of ships. Akila sat, watching while the ships under his command scattered and hunted, harried and ran. They drew their targets away from the main body of the fleet, only this time, they didn't swarm together to attack the vessels they'd lured away. This time, they kept running, drawing more ships and pulling them further out.

All the while, Akila held the galley in position, its oarsmen poised, forcing himself to wait even though there were ships that could have used his help. Even though there was a rebel ship burning now in the distance. There would only be one chance to get this right.

He saw it then. The flagship of Felldust's fleet came into view, appearing from behind walls of other vessels as they broke away to attack his fleet. They scattered like hounds chasing after rabbits, and in doing so, they left their leader exposed.

"Row!" Akila ordered, and his men were more than equal to the task. The galley powered forward, cutting through what had once been an impenetrable wall of ships to strike at what lay beyond.

Akila wasn't naïve enough to believe that killing the First Stone of Felldust would end the invasion like magic. This wasn't a case where cutting off the snake's head would kill the body, but it might slow things. It might cause the invasion to fragment as the different factions there found themselves fighting for control of the fleet. Without a leader, it might not scatter to the four winds, but it would split into smaller things they could deal with.

"Maybe I can even declare myself First Stone," Akila said with a laugh. That was how things worked there, wasn't it? The strongest took the ruler's seat. "Maybe I could just order them all to go home."

Somehow, Akila doubted that it would work like that. He wasn't even sure that he was going to survive this. He could kill Irrien though. The first impact from the galley's ram would tear through the hull of his flagship, and they could pull back to give him to the water, picking him and his men off at will as they tried to flee the sinking ship.

Akila stood as close to the prow as he dared right then. The galley was a giant spear, and he was its point, ready to slam home in Irrien's heart. He drew his short swords, ready to fight…

And that was when he saw Irrien's flagship start to shift in the water.

It turned, and if Akila had thought it would be ponderously slow, he was wrong. It turned with all the speed of his own ship, and Akila hesitated at the thought that it was heading straight for him now, not trying to get away, but charging.

Akila's head snapped around to give the order to break off. A good commander thought on his feet. They'd missed this moment, but there would be another, and another, until finally he found the chance to make this tactic work. They needed to break for open water, maybe help one of the distracting ships.

But as he looked around, Akila saw the ships that were closing in from other directions. The ones that had been chasing his ships had broken off, and were skimming their way back in toward the flagship while the rebellion's ships continued to run.

Akila had thought that he was thrusting at the heart of Felldust's fleet. Now, it was more like he was running into the palm of its hand, and its fingers were coming in to crush him. The First Stone had outthought him. He'd left an opening, and Akila had charged in like a novice on his first day of sword practice, to be rapped on the head while he went for too easy a thrust.

In a real fight, though, that kind of thing could still work. Just so long as you made sure your attack struck home too, and you were prepared to pay the price.

"Keep going," Akila ordered. "We're going to take them with us, if nothing else! Get ready to board!"

The galley and the flagship continued on their collision course. Ramming was out. The only question now was which way to go. Which way would the First Stone choose when the time came to turn? Would he turn at all? No, Akila decided. He would plow on, the determined warrior relying on the strength of his ship.

That meant Akila could pick his side.

"Port rowers, be ready to ship oars. Tillermen, be ready to go hard starboard. Soldiers ready on the port side."

For a moment or two, there was a scramble as his men hurried to their positions. The sailors who weren't going to be in the first rush of battle found rails to brace themselves against, guessing what he was planning.

Akila waited as long as he dared. Finally, he couldn't leave it any longer.

"Now!" he yelled. "Ship oars. Hard starboard!"

It was a risky move, but potentially a decisive one when fighting with galleys. If you couldn't ram, you scraped down the side of the enemy's ship and tore away their oars with your hull to leave them limping. That made it easy to attack from an angle they couldn't defend.

Except that even as he called the attack, he saw the hooked spikes on the sides of the Felldust flagship. He saw it pulling in its own oars. It was ready for this, and if they didn't pull away—

The thought cut off in the crash of wood against wood. It was a collision in slow motion, but even so, the impact made Akila fall to one knee as the hooks tore into his ship, ripping at it as they went past one another. They gouged into the oar banks of his ship, and Akila heard men screaming.

The ship seemed to scream too, in the groan and crack of wood pushed beyond its breaking point; in lines that snapped and iron plates that buckled. The whistle of arrows joined those sounds as the two ships' crews shot at one another, and Akila ducked out of the way as one struck the deck beside him.

As quickly as they'd come together, the ships were past one another, but that brought no relief with it. Akila could feel the galley beneath him listing in the water, the whole thing tilting and rolling as it struggled to recover from the impact.

"Bring us to bear!" he yelled, hoping that someone was listening. "Bring us around or we're dead!"

It made no difference. Akila could give all the orders he wanted, but the ship and its crew just weren't capable of making it happen. He didn't know how many oars they'd lost, or how many men. However many it was, it was too many. They were trying to turn, but now the fight was like a man weighed down with heavy sacks trying to keep up with a duelist. It was the kind of fight Akila had always tried to have, but now he was on the wrong side of it.

He watched Irrien's flagship turn, as gracefully as a blade-covered swan. It spun toward his ship, and now it was lined up to strike amidships. Akila's galley was turning, but it could never do it fast enough.

He saw the ram of the flagship bearing down on them, and all Akila could do was brace for the inevitable, crushing impact. All he could do now was try to die well.

That, and take Irrien with him.

CHAPTER FIFTEEN

The others on his flagship braced against whatever they could grab while they rammed the enemy's galley, but Irrien remained impassive in his throne. He would not let others see him clinging to the mast like some weakling. He was strong, and in moments, he would be victorious.

He had a moment to savor the way he'd drawn in his enemy. This foe had been a cunning one, worrying at the edges of his fleet the way wolves hounded the edges of a herd. He'd forgotten, though, that Irrien was not some deer or cattle to be brought down. He was a fighting man, well used to such tactics. The folk of the dust had fought that way for years.

Irrien had been patient. He'd let his enemy's confidence grow. Then he'd left his opening. Now he smiled. He enjoyed the moment when he outthought an enemy. When it came to the politics of the city, he loved watching their faces when they realized that some plot had failed. He loved watching their hope fade.

There was a place for all of that, but there was a place for violence too. For proving yourself the stronger, the deadlier, the more able. Irrien drew his sword and waited.

The impact of the collision was like the shaking of a mountain, making the boards beneath Irrien's feet rumble and knocking some of his slaves sprawling. His flagship plunged into the galley like a sword through the side of a foe, then held to it, as tightly as a lover. It would need to pull back soon so that the weight of the ruined vessel didn't drag them all down, but for now, there was killing to be done.

"Attack!" Irrien ordered, and the violence began.

He watched arrows rain down, from his men and those of the enemy who hadn't been knocked down. He saw a spear flung between the ships, thrown by one of his crew who fancied himself an expert with it. Irrien snorted. An expert did not throw away his weapon.

He stayed seated as the first warriors leapt between the two ships. There were those who leapt from the enemy galley: rats leaving their sinking ship or brave men eager to take the fight to an enemy. He saw a sailor leap with a long knife clutched in one hand, grabbing onto the rigging of Irrien's ship as he sought to leave his stricken vessel. He saw a warrior wearing mail leap across the gap between the two only to be pushed back, tumbling down into the water below.

"Fool," Irrien said softly. The word was quickly lost in the sounds of the battle.

His own men leapt onto the enemy ship, using lines and hooks to pull it close enough to make the leap. There were always those who sought to impress Irrien with their bravery and their eagerness. Irrien even encouraged them, offering coin and better spoil shares to those who were the first to scale walls or board ships. He did it because they were invariably the first to die, and lesser men had to be given the illusion that it was worth it. A good leader knew when to buy loyalty and when to command it. Oh, and when to use fear. Any man seen to be holding back would suffer for it.

Irrien was not holding back. He was letting the battle bloom like a flower before plucking, or wine left before drinking. Some pleasures were better when taken at their peak. So he sat and watched as one of his warriors clove through the collar bone of a foe with an axe; as an enemy cut him down in turn with rapid thrusts of a knife.

The chaos spread, and Irrien set his sword across his knees, waiting for the perfect moment. He watched a foe impaled on a spiked shield, scrabbling at the edges and trying to thrust over it with a short sword. He saw a slave woman get in the way of the violence, cut down by a backhand sweep of a sword. Irrien cursed the waste there, and the stupidity of the woman for getting in the way in the first place.

He saw a man leap across with a blade in either hand. He was scarred and whip lean, moving like water through the violence around him, his blades singing with every clash of steel.

Irrien watched him and knew without being told that this was Akila. He'd learned to read men by watching them fight, learning about them in the only arena where a man couldn't hide what he was. He watched Akila, and Irrien liked what he saw. This was a man who was direct, but not foolish, quick thinking, but not flighty. When Akila parried blows meant for others, Irrien saw that he cared about his men. When he commanded them even as he fought, Irrien saw the ability to keep a clear head in the chaos.

A foe worth killing, then.

Irrien stood, taking his long blade in both hands. His slaves stepped back from him as he let his cloak fall. He stilled himself, checking the angle of the sun so that he wouldn't be blinded by it as he fought.

Then he strode forward and started killing.

There were probably men for whom fighting was hard. For whom it was a rush of emotions and needs cluttering the simple beauty of the violence. Irrien didn't feel that. There was a sea of cold rage flooding through his limbs, yet he floated above it, directing and reacting with the speed that had always been his gift despite his size.

He swept his sword around in an arc that smashed through a man's shield, taking half the arm beneath. He deflected a sword blow with the cross guard of his sword, then struck out with the pommel, feeling bone break.

He spun, cutting upward to hack through a man's leg, ducked an attack, then threw one foe into another. He paused for a moment, listening to the clash of blades as if trying to hear the song within, then plunged back into the fray.

He'd always been a skilled warrior. In his tribe, they had reckoned his father stronger, until the day Irrien had killed him. He'd honed his skills then, through years of war and the challenges of the city. He'd had combatlords brought from the pits of the Empire to teach him more, and blade masters from a dozen different lands. Always, he'd had them poisoned when he was done, to make sure that they could tell no one of any weaknesses they saw.

No man could hope to stand against him now.

They tried, though, as Irrien cut his way across the deck of his ship, aiming for the spot where the rebels' leader fought. Akila danced his way from enemy to enemy, slicing and moving, never still. Already, Irrien found himself planning for the fight ahead, and that was dangerous. He felt a sword glance from the armor he wore, trapped it with his blade and thrust through a man.

Space started to open up around him as men kept back from the swings of his sword. That was to Irrien's advantage. It meant that he could see attacks coming, and could pick his targets one by one. His long arms and strong frame meant that he could close the distance quickly, picking out a sailor and striking him down before he could even raise his sword.

Twice more, Irrien struck, each time picking the weakest looking of the foes around him, each time cutting them down with savage blows that carved right through their flesh. He kept his blade sharp.

"Enjoying taking out men who can't give you a good fight?" Akila asked, stepping into the space that Irrien had opened up with his blade.

Irrien shrugged. As he'd thought, Akila's attachment to his men was a weapon to turn against him. Every weakness could be exploited. A man who did not understand this deserved to die.

Irrien struck out first, although he didn't commit, the way many large men might have. He was already anticipating Akila's evasion, although the rebel leader surprised him by springing forward, not dodging sideways. Irrien had to spring back, barely avoiding the blow.

"You're fast," he said, with a grim smile. "That's good. A man should have foes worth killing."

"Well, I don't know about that," Akila shot back. "But until one shows up, I'll settle for killing you."

Irrien ignored that. Weak men allowed themselves to be goaded.

He parried as Akila sprang forward, the rebel's twin blades seemingly everywhere at once. Irrien blocked three strikes, dodged a fourth, and kicked out to force Akila back. He tried a lateral sweep of his sword, which Akila ducked, then cut low so that the man had to jump.

"You dance well," Irrien said, and cut halfway through saying it, aiming to take his foe by surprise. There were no rules in war. In truth, Irrien only obeyed those in the rest of life because they helped to get him what he wanted.

Akila parried the strike with his blades crossed, and Irrien felt the impact of it. The other man circled then, keeping his distance and darting in for strikes. He feinted high and cut low. Irrien went to parry, and Akila came back high again. Irrien jerked his head back, but felt the tip of the blade nick his jaw.

He attacked then. Speed and cunning counted, but so did strength, and Irrien had that in abundance. He cut and cut, forcing Akila to move, to block, to dodge. Irrien wore his foe down, while around him the battle raged. He saw an opening to attack, and in that moment two warriors stumbled into their way, struggling over a hatchet.

Irrien cut them both down, not caring that one of them was his follower. No one kept him from a death he had claimed.

He went back to chasing Akila. The rebel leader probably thought that he was wearing Irrien down, but Irrien could fight for hours if he had to. Even so...

He let his blade drag a little, as if the weight of the great sword were too much. He even let a shallow cut through, allowing it to scrape along his arm, only partly parried. He feigned a stumble.

"Really?" Akila demanded, lowering his weapons. "You caught me with that trick once with your fleet, remember? I'm not—"

Irrien lunged then, snake fast and deadly. He'd guessed that his opponent wouldn't take the bait. He'd guessed that he would lower his guard. Always being that extra step ahead was what won fights.

It won this one. Irrien felt the moment when his sword struck home, plunging deep into Akila.

Irrien had a moment to savor that victory—until he realized that Akila was pulling himself forward, along the blade, moving closer. What kind of strength did it take to do that? What kind of insanity did it take to do it just for the sake of some cause?

Akila suddenly lashed out, and Irrien shrieked despite himself, feeling pain blossom in his shoulder as Akila's sword bit home. The wound was deep.

Irrien was stunned.

"You won't win," Akila said.

"Of course we will," Irrien replied.

Irrien rallied and kicked the sword from Akila's hands.

He heard Akila gasp with pain as he shoved his own sword deeper.

"Ceres… will stop you," Akila gasped.

Irrien shook his head.

"I thank you," he said. "You were a worthy foe."

He stepped forward and kicked Akila from the ship, his long blade still embedded in him, and watched him plunge overboard, into the murky, bloody waters.

"But not worthy enough."

CHAPTER SIXTEEN

Stephania was serene as she made her way to the Hall of Knowledge, gliding as the elegant heart of a coterie of guards and handmaidens, nobles and spies. She'd always seen the value of information, and this was the place where she could find out almost anything she wanted.

She just hoped that it held answers that could save her child.

Some of the nobles looked as though they hadn't walked so much in years, and Stephania smiled a little at forcing them to make the effort. It was good for a ruler to keep those around her a little uncomfortable.

A ruler. Stephania didn't get tired of thinking that. When she'd been just a noble, Stephania had assumed that royalty was a tiny step, and it was, but it was more than that. It was a shift in state, taking her from being one of the foremost of a group of peers to something different. Something special. She could order any one of them executed on a whim, and they knew it.

"How are the defenses progressing?" Stephania asked.

The guard captain, *her* guard captain, stepped forward. "There is nothing to worry about, your majesty. Everything is in hand. The invaders will not get to us in here."

He said it the way Stephania might have reassured some young noble girl worried about her first feast. She held her anger in check, because she couldn't afford to alienate the man. In that sense, being a ruler wasn't so different. Even a queen still required the support of others, the control of opinion and the power bought through loyalty. Queen Athena had forgotten that. Stephania wouldn't.

"I am not looking for reassurances," Stephania said. "I require details. I know our efforts in the tunnels have been successful, but what of the rest?"

The guard captain looked a little surprised, but nodded. "We have reinforced the gates with iron bars," he said, "and set boiling sand above them. An enemy without a key would die long before he broke through. The walls have been checked for defects, and we have set nets to catch fire arrows."

It did sound as though they could keep enemies out for weeks if necessary. Stephania knew that they had stores. She'd checked on them herself.

"Elethe, what about our agents?"

"We have recruited some within the city using the promise of food and shelter if they give us valuable information," her handmaiden said. "Lydia and Nerine are questioning Queen Athena's former servants to see if any might be suitable to join us."

Questioning was probably a polite word for some of it. Stephania had taught her handmaidens to be ruthless.

"What about beyond the Empire?" she asked. "The war will pass, but then we must be well placed to continue our relations with others. We must have information."

"Birds have been sent," Elethe replied. "With the invasion, it is hard to do more."

Yet there was always more that could be done. Stephania turned to the nobles in the contingent with her.

"If you have relatives beyond the borders of the Empire," she said, "make use of them. Write to them. Use whatever birds you need. Frame it as asking for news, and I'm sure they will tell us all we need to know. Tell them that I will offer coin for informers they find."

She snapped her fingers at another of her handmaidens. "We will need messengers to send to the invaders, starting to negotiate the peace. Tell them that they may take what they wish from the city, but that when they tire of battering in vain against the castle walls, we will be ready to talk."

Of course, considering what the First Stone would probably do to the messengers, it probably wasn't worth wasting good people on it.

"Send those of Queen Athena's people who wish to prove themselves," Stephania said. "Although make sure that they don't know anything too important first."

Whatever they did know, they would undoubtedly tell the invaders. Felldust's torturers were rumored to be very inventive. Stephania thought of the girl she was preparing to play the part of her. If Irrien saw through the disguise, or if he had no interest in talking, that girl would die. Stephania felt a hint of guilt at that, but not much. You looked after yourself first, your family second, and those beyond only after that.

The thought of that brought her attention to the Hall of Knowledge. The doors were shut for once, and Stephania was impressed by the way they muffled some of the cries from within.

"Elethe, with me," she commanded. "The rest of you, wait here."

When she stepped inside, Stephania had to admit that she was a little disappointed. She liked things to be neat, and things in here were anything but that. There were papers strewn everywhere, several with blood on them. Old Cosmas sat tied to a chair, with blood on his face, and on his hands where the two handmaidens beside him had torn out his fingernails. One side of his face was bruised until he barely resembled the scholar he had been.

Stephania made a small sound of disappointment as she looked at her handmaidens. They stared at her in surprise, then quickly knelt.

"I sent you to gain information," Stephania said, "not to cause chaos."

"Forgive us, your majesty," the older of the two said. "But he would not talk to us. He called you a false queen, and he didn't respond to threats or promises. When Ustra offered herself to him, he laughed."

"And so you beat him bloody as a side of beef," Stephania said, letting the disappointment creep into her voice. "Go, both of you. We'll find you tasks more suited to your talents."

They left, at a speed that suggested they knew exactly how lucky they were to be allowed to do so.

Stephania found a chair for herself, sitting beside Cosmas and putting a hand over his. Of course, given his injuries, that just made the old man whimper in pain.

"Please forgive my handmaidens, Cosmas," she said. "They have such a limited idea of how to do things. They don't understand that the goal is to get information, not just to gratify their need for pain. If it helps, I will be having both of them whipped for their mistake later."

"You... are worse than both of them," Cosmas replied. "The philosopher Caxin tells us that we cannot blame a snake for biting—"

"But we can blame the one who puts it in your bed," Stephania finished for him. "Yes, I have read his work. I didn't find him very convincing. Oh, is that a surprise, Cosmas? You always did give me such condescending looks when I came in here. Did you think I was just looking at ancient dress designs, or reading the parts of *the ten thousand pleasures* I shouldn't have been?"

She'd done both, of course. For a young noblewoman, both were weapons to use against enemies, and of course, she'd done a good job of pretending to be harmless.

"I'm more surprised you weren't reading the tomes on poisons," Cosmas said.

"Ah, so you *did* know what I was like," Stephania replied, even though she didn't really believe it. It was better to flatter sometimes. Better to let people go on thinking that they were the clever ones, until it was too late. "Wise old Cosmas, who sees all and knows all, then tells people whatever he thinks they need to know. Tell me, old man, whose side are you on?"

Even tied and beaten, he managed to give Stephania a look that said she would never understand.

"On the side of the Empire," Cosmas said. "On the side of doing what was best for *all* of it, not just a few nobles, or a few rebels. Since you know so much of the philosophers, you will have heard Xin Lu's contention that a man must make his own morality and stick to it."

Stephania had read it. It had seemed to her to be more wasted air. You did what you could in this world for your own benefit, because you knew that everyone else would be doing the same.

"Well," Stephania said, "as a man who hears everything, you will have heard that I rule the Empire now. As its queen, I command your obedience."

"Queen of a castle about to be taken," Cosmas countered. "Queen, not by right, but by violence."

Elethe stepped forward to strike Cosmas. Stephania stopped her with a gesture. It wasn't mercy. It was simply that she couldn't afford for the old man to die before he'd told her all he knew.

"All rulers rule through violence," Stephania said. "The kindest king will hang those who rise against him, or see his throne taken. As for right... I thought I was married to the Empire's rightful heir?"

She enjoyed the shock on Cosmas's face.

"Oh, I know about Thanos. I don't suppose you have proof for me, do you? It might come in useful."

Cosmas sat in silence.

"This is unwise, Cosmas," Stephania said.

"You're going to torture me some more?" he shot back.

Stephania shook her head. Instead, she stood, looking around until she found a slim volume, cracked with age.

"One of the philosophers you love so much," she said. "Presumably very rare?"

"Irreplaceable," Cosmas replied.

Stephania smiled at that, then started to rip out pages.

"No," Cosmas said. "What are you doing?"

Stephania looked over at Elethe while she continued to tear out pages. "The key to getting what you want from someone is to understand what they hold dear. It *might* be their well-being, in which case pain and threats will work. It might be their children, or their position... or the books they've spent a lifetime accumulating. Fetch a brazier, would you? I think it will be easier to burn things."

"No!" Cosmas said, tearing at his bonds as if he might escape the chair that held him. "You can't!"

Stephania tore out another page. "I can, and I will. You will watch me destroy every book here, unless you start to tell me what I want to know."

She got through three more pages before Cosmas broke. Stephania raised an eyebrow. She'd expected it to be more.

"Thanos is mentioned in a genealogy," Cosmas said. "He's there as the king's son."

That was a start, although Stephania definitely wouldn't leave it there.

"I will need more than that," Stephania said. She held up the book by way of emphasis.

"There was… there was talk that Thanos's mother had moved on," Cosmas replied. "The rumors said to Felldust, but I… there were letters. Somewhere in here, there are letters."

"Where?" Stephania demanded.

Cosmas shook his head. "I don't know the location of everything here, only that they *are* here. Or they were. I put them in a box somewhere."

That sounded like Cosmas. All the information in the world, and he couldn't find half of it. Stephania decided to move on to the one thing she wanted to know about even more.

"What do you know about sorcerers?" Stephania asked.

She saw Cosmas swallow. "There are many things written about them. I have accounts—"

Stephania waved that away. "There was a sorcerer in Felldust. Daskalos. I need to know about his weaknesses. I made a deal with him, and I need to know how to undo it."

She saw Cosmas pale slightly, and knew he'd heard the name.

"I cannot help you," Cosmas said.

"Elethe, fetch that brazier," Stephania commanded. This time, her handmaiden rushed to obey. Stephania clamped her hand down over Cosmas's, ignoring his cry of pain. "You think I won't carry out my threats? You think I won't burn your precious scrolls? You will tell me what you know. I will save my child!"

"You promised him your child?" Cosmas said. He shook his head. "You are a fool. A man like Daskalos cannot be cheated."

"Then I'll kill him," Stephania said, although even as she said it, she found herself thinking of the way he'd come back from her knife thrust in the cave. "I will find a way."

"There *is* no way," Cosmas said. "I've read about him, in books so old that with any other man I would have thought it was a successor or a student now. They say that he has the secret of hiding his life in an object, and unless you destroy that, he cannot be killed. That he can use the wind to listen and the refection on a pool to see. How do you fight such a man?"

"That is what I want you to tell me," Stephania said. She could feel the anger rising in her now. She tried to be reasonable, but people never did what they were supposed to.

Cosmas laughed then. He laughed long and loud, even as Stephania threw his precious book against the nearest wall, scattering its pages.

"Look at you," he said. "You're right, everyone has something they care about. For me, yes, it's my books. For you, though… you've given away the one thing that matters to you, you stupid girl. You had a life with Thanos, you had a child on the way, and you gave it all up. You can't stop Daskalos, and I'll laugh when he takes the one thing that matters from you."

"No you won't," Stephania assured him. She took a knife from her belt. "I'm sick of your interference, Cosmas. I'm sick of you hoarding other people's secrets to hand out like sweetmeats. I'm sick of you pretending to know everything, and do you know the thing about being a queen?"

Cosmas might have started to answer, but Stephania stepped forward, thrusting her blade up under his ribs.

"The thing about being a queen is that you don't have to listen to people who anger you," she said. "You can just *deal* with them."

She watched Cosmas die. There was probably a time when she would have felt something at seeing the light go out of the old scholar's eyes. Now, she was just happy that he wouldn't be interfering in her business any longer.

When Elethe came with the brazier, Stephania saw her hesitate before setting it down and dropping to one knee.

"My queen?"

Stephania imagined how she must look then, with blood on her hands. Idly, she wiped her hands on the remains of one of Cosmas's scrolls.

"I got tired of waiting. Remove his body, then have the others go through this place from top to bottom. There are letters here I want to find."

"Yes, your majesty." Elethe sounded frightened then. That caught Stephania a little by surprise.

"You don't need to be afraid of me," Stephania said. "You're serving me well. Come find me when you're done here."

"Yes, your majesty. Where should I find you?"

There was only one answer to that.

"With Ceres. As I said, everything has a breaking point. I intend to find hers."

CHAPTER SEVENTEEN

Thanos dreamed, and in his dreams, the dead stared at him. He saw people he'd known, people he'd fought, people he'd been forced to kill. He saw his brother and his father, fighting in front of the statues of his ancestors that lined the royal chambers. A second later, the statues were replaced by figures who stood there, ancestors looking at him in accusation, in recognition, and very occasionally in respect.

"Are you really here?" Thanos asked. "What is this?"

His father didn't answer. Nor did Lucious. They kept fighting in front of those who had gone before, rolling on the floor as new figures started to emerge from spaces in the walls.

The Bone Folk stepped up next to Thanos's ancestors, and one by one, he saw them start to devour them. They drank down the ghosts like smoke, taking them in huge gulps that left nothing behind. When they turned to his father and Lucious, Thanos wanted to do something, but he couldn't move…

He woke to the rocking of the ship that was carrying him to Delos. Thanos sat up and saw Jeva crouched a little way away, her eyes fixed on him. After the dream he'd just had, that was a little unnerving.

"You look as though you're trying to decide whether to eat me," Thanos said.

She gave him a grim look, and when she spoke, it was in tones of obvious insult. "You know it does not work like that for us."

"I'm sorry."

"Besides," she continued with a laugh, "you'd be far too stringy."

Thanos laughed with her. He wasn't sure he could even begin to understand the Bone Folk woman. They'd been traveling together for days, and Thanos still wasn't sure he was any closer to being able to read Jeva.

It seemed she could read him though.

"The dead can be difficult sometimes," she said.

"Did you see something?" Thanos asked.

She spread her hands. It wasn't an answer, but it seemed as though Jeva wasn't one to give out answers. It was enough that her people had agreed to help.

"Do I look like a seer, to see into your dreams?" she asked. "I just know that look. What did you dream of?"

"Of someone I cared about. Of the dead being eaten."

Thanos couldn't think of a better way to put it.

"That is a good thing," Jeva said. "It reminds us of our connection to them. We are the tip of a spear that goes back lifetimes."

Thanos wished that he could see things that way. Maybe he wouldn't feel quite so alone then. That thought made him think of Ceres. He would get back to her. Right then, he wanted to get back to her more than anything else in the world, but it felt as though every step he took was a frustration, leading him into more problems, and pulling him further from her.

It didn't help that the Bone Folk's fleet was a strange thing that looked as though it should barely have floated. Each of their ships incorporated as many of the bones of great beasts as the rest of their architecture, so that ribs taken from whales wrapped around their hulls, and shark teeth formed arrow tips as they prepared for war. It was a terrifying-looking fleet, and a part of Thanos still wasn't sure if he should be bringing these people to the shores of Delos. What if he was just making things worse?

Even the smugglers who had taken him to Port Leeward kept their distance from the main body of the fleet, as though unwilling to risk having the Bone Folk too close. When Thanos had declared that he would be traveling on one of their ships, the captain had looked at him as though he was mad. Yet Thanos had done it. He knew he needed to show his new allies that he trusted them. Strangely, he *did* trust them.

And they were willing to help. That counted for a lot.

In the distance, Thanos thought he saw ships. He hurried to the railing, trying to ignore the bone feel of it under his hands.

"They are the stragglers of Felldust's fleet," Jeva said, coming up beside him so quietly that Thanos was glad she wasn't his enemy. "They head to the city like gulls upon a carcass. Would you like us to destroy them?"

Thanos looked around. They had the ships to do it. The Bone Folk had an impressive fleet of ships thanks to their years of piracy. Even so, if they went into combat with a convoy like that, the odds were that they would suffer losses.

Thanos shook his head.

"It's better not to," he said. "I don't want to get into any fights we don't need before we get there."

"That is what we thought," Jeva said. "We are going to your Ceres's aid. Better not to waste our efforts on lesser things."

His Ceres. Thanos wished it were as simple as that. That things between them hadn't been so difficult when he left. With everything that he'd done, and everything that Stephania had managed to insinuate, Thanos wasn't sure that they'd ever been further apart. He only hoped that he could change that by showing her how much he was prepared to do to keep her safe.

He was prepared to bring a fleet of the most feared pirates of Felldust to attack its fleet, for one thing.

Yet, the more he looked at the fleet the Bone Folk had assembled, the more worried he got. They would have suffered losses taking on a fragment of the fleet that Felldust could bring to bear. How would they fare against the whole thing? Thanos had seen some of the ships for that. He'd seen the vessels stretching across Port Leeward's harbor, and those were just the ones trying to catch up. How huge would the main force be?

More to the point, how could they ever hope to stand against it? What if they reached the fleet, attacked it, and found that it was like adding a single drop of wine to a barrel of water? They might be overwhelmed and destroyed so quickly that it was as though they weren't there at all.

"You're worrying," Jeva said.

Thanos nodded. "I am. I've seen you fight. I've heard your reputations as pirates, and the fact that the First Stone wanted you to join the invasion says a lot about how dangerous you are as warriors…"

"But?" Jeva prompted.

She sounded as though she'd been waiting for this moment. Perhaps she had. Thanos was quickly learning not to underestimate the people he traveled with.

"We might not win," Thanos said. "I've brought you all this way, and I might be sending you to your deaths. Felldust's fleet is going to be huge. So big that we might not be able to beat it even if we take it by surprise."

He watched as Jeva cocked her head to one side.

"And you're telling me this because…"

"Because I want to be fair," Thanos said. "I want to give you the chance to pull out of this if you want to. You and all your people."

Jeva nodded gravely. She turned back to the rest of the ship and started to speak in the strange dialect her people had. It seemed to bear no connection to the main tongue of Felldust, with clicks and sharp edges to the words that made it sound almost like bone scraping against bone.

"I am telling them that we might not win," she said. "That you wanted them to know this. That it was very important to you to say this."

Then she burst out laughing. So, to Thanos's surprise, did most of the others on the ship. They treated the whole thing as if it were the best joke they'd heard in a long time. One of the sailors actually leaned against the bleached mast of the ship as though he had trouble keeping his footing, he was laughing that much.

"We *know* we won't win," Jeva said. "I saw the fleet myself. You think I can't *count*?"

"No," Thanos said. "I just—"

"You just thought that you could find a way through all this without anyone dying. We're not afraid of dying. Going to join our ancestors? For us, it means finally getting a say in how things go."

Thanos wasn't sure that he could wrap his mind around that. All the other people he'd met cared whether they lived or died, even if occasionally they felt that a cause, or another person, was worth the risk.

"We came here knowing what would happen," Jeva went on. "The ones who speak to the dead say that it is a thing worth doing. More than that, we *know* it is worth doing. We have stories about the Ancient Ones. We know how important they were to the world, and how important they might still be."

Thanos found it strange that Ceres's name could inspire so much, even though he knew that she was more than worth any risk in person. These people had never met her, but they were willing to die for her.

"We will strike at their fleet," Jeva said. "We will punch a hole through them, and perhaps in that hole, you will be able to get the Ancient One to safety. We will do what is necessary."

Thanos didn't know what to say to that. Should he thank them for what they were doing, or would they see that as another joke? Worse, would they see it as an insult? Thanos was starting to realize that he didn't know them at all, but that didn't matter. Not when they were prepared to do this.

Looking out, he saw land appearing on the horizon. The Empire lay ahead, with all the conflict that would follow. In the distance, Thanos thought he saw fires, and fear gripped him then. What if they were too late? What if the conflict was already over?

"You should go back to the other boat," Jeva said. "You do not want to be on this one when the battle starts, and we wouldn't want to get your bones mixed up with those of our people when it is done."

"Thank you," Thanos said.

Jeva shook her head. "Do not thank us. Do what must be done. And when the time comes, remember to die well!"

CHAPTER EIGHTEEN

Irrien smiled in grim satisfaction as his flagship scraped up against Delos's docks. With the enemy fleet in tatters, it had been an easy thing to break the harbor chain and pour into the space behind like a stain on the water. He felt the deep rightness of things going as he had planned them.

Flaming missiles flew over his head, but Irrien didn't duck. A leader couldn't afford to show weakness. Especially not a First Stone. Irrien had taken his position by defeating the last holder of the seat, seizing his interests and finally slaying him. His men liked to profess their loyalty, but he knew there was always someone, somewhere, who would try to take it from him if they felt that they could.

So he stood tall, ignoring the pain in his arm where Akila had wounded him, ignoring the flight of the fire arrows and the clay pots that hissed with oil when they struck the water. Ignoring even the thought that victory was in his grasp. A strong man did not let what was to be gained distract him from the process of seizing it.

"Forward!" Irrien called. "Take the docks!"

He followed the first wave of men down onto them, drawing a knife so long that for another man it would have been a short sword. He was grateful in that moment that he'd thought to leave his great sword in Akila when he'd kicked him down for the sharks to take. A blade could be replaced easily enough; a reputation was a more difficult thing.

Irrien saw a rebel coming at him through the throng of the battle, holding an axe. He sidestepped the man's attack, striking out with his knife at throat level. He let the attacker drop, sheathed his knife, and took up the axe with his good hand.

"The first victory on Empire soil!" Irrien called, hefting it overhead. He didn't raise his left arm. He wasn't sure that he could. No doubt his healers would be able to help, but for now, he wanted that aura of invincibility.

Around him, his men hacked and killed, spurred on by Irrien's display. They tore into the defenders around the docks, fighting their way to the spots where two catapults continued to fling flaming pots toward Irrien's fleet.

Men trying to be brave. Irrien didn't know whether to be impressed or to laugh.

He did neither, instead settling for smashing his axe through the skull of another foe, then using it to sweep aside the head of a spear so that he could cut into its wielder.

"Kill the men on those catapults," Irrien called, "but do not destroy them. Inside the harbor, they can protect *us*."

His warriors hastened to obey. Irrien saw a woman in the wraps of one of the dust tribes plunge a short spear into a rebel. He watched as one of the spike-haired gang members of Port Leeward jumped in with a knife in either hand. War brought people together the way almost nothing else could.

Away to his left, Irrien saw a collection of people with their belongings on their backs, scuttling through the streets like the rats they were as they tried to flee. Men and women, even a few children. Irrien looked around and saw that the battle for the docks was going well.

Well enough for him to take a detour.

"All of you here, with me," Irrien said, and ran in the direction of the fleeing people. He sprinted along the front of the docks, leading a small group of his warriors who bayed for blood like sand lizards.

He saw the tripwire just in time.

"Halt!" he yelled, skidding to a stop, but some of those with him were too slow to react, or hadn't heard him, or were too caught up in their need for blood to listen. Whatever the reason, several sprinted past him, hitting the line of tripwires as a group.

Bolts flew out from crossbows connected to them, thudding as they slammed into flesh. Irrien saw a muscled man with the bearskin cloak of one of the Dead Forest tribes go down, looking surprised at the thought that death might have come for him. A warrior in light chain found that it was no match for the force of the weapon coming toward her.

Irrien had to admire the mind that had put these traps in place. A man could not live with such things around, but this was not about living with them; it was about denying the city to those who attacked, whatever the cost.

"Careful," Irrien said. "There will be more."

There were. As they advanced, he spotted wires linked to barricades holding rubble. He found deadfalls and pits, spikes and more crossbows. Every step seemed to be fraught with danger, but Irrien picked his way through it.

Those trying to flee were still ahead, and Irrien wasn't going to let the weak escape so easily.

He saw them ahead and charged after them. His followers charged with him. Irrien slammed into the back of them, cutting down one of the men. Another turned, trying to draw a knife, and Irrien hacked at him with his axe. He ignored the spray of blood, looking for another foe to kill.

There were none, though, because these folk would not fight for their lives. They just cowered there like the slaves they would soon be. Half of them were already on their knees, and Irrien found himself sorting them in his mind. The young women and the few strong men who would fetch the best price. The older women and the boys. The rest. Some they would keep for now. Some they would put on oars. One woman with dark hair, Irrien decided that he would keep for himself, until she bored him enough to sell or give to the priests for one of their sacrifices.

He strode to her, standing over her, seeing the fear in her eyes.

"Tell me, who set the traps in the street?" Irrien demanded.

She looked up at him with obvious terror, and Irrien thought he might have to strike her to get her talking. But the words came blurting out, as they always did from those without the strength to fight.

"There is a man named Berin," the woman said. "Ceres's father. He and his smiths came through the streets, building defenses."

"And did any here help him?" Irrien demanded.

She shook her head frantically. "No. We didn't want to be involved in their war. We wanted… we wanted to be safe."

The bleating of the lamb in the field, as it always was. Please don't hurt us. As if words could do anything to stop one with strength. Perhaps this one thought that she'd done something right by admitting that she hadn't even tried to defend what was hers.

"And Ceres is in the castle, waiting for us?" Irrien asked.

The woman shook her head. "No, I mean… maybe. They say that Lady Stephania took the castle back from the rebellion. That she captured Ceres."

Irrien considered that. It was an interesting development. He had heard of Lady Stephania, for one thing. It was said that her beauty outshone the stars, while her cunning left men dead in its wake. A woman to admire, in other words.

Still, it made no difference who sat within the castle. Irrien intended to take it, as he would the rest of the city. His new slave's words merely changed the nature of the prize, not what had to be done.

"You will tell me everything you know of this Lady Stephania," he said.

"I might be able to help you with that," a woman's voice replied. She stepped from the shadows of one of the houses, moving quietly enough that even Irrien hadn't spotted her coming. That was the kind of silence that took training.

She was comely enough, and nobly dressed beneath a dark cloak that was no doubt designed to disguise who she was while she made her way through the city.

"Lady Stephania sent me, my lord," she said, with a curtsey that was probably fit for a king in this uncivilized land where the weak did not kneel before their betters. "My name is Wanale."

"Were you sent as a messenger, a gift, or an assassin?" Irrien demanded.

"As a messenger, my lord," Wanale said. "Lady Stephania wishes to offer you terms."

Irrien laughed at that, even as his mind considered the possibilities. He'd heard the stories of the times Lady Stephania had manipulated people into doing what she wanted. She had done a good job of seeming harmless and then striking.

"What terms could she have that I would want?" Irrien said. "I will take the city. I will take all that I want. She has nothing to give."

"She told me to say that she has the potential to take from you," Wanale said. "That the castle will remain strong, and that failing against it will make you look weak. That it is better to agree terms than to watch your forces fight among themselves when they cannot take the castle."

Irrien looked at the messenger until she quailed and fell to her knees. That was good. A man should have enough strength to cow lesser folk.

"All of this assumes that I cannot take what is in front of me," Irrien said. He took a step toward the woman. "You will find out that is not the case with my slave chains on you. Then you will tell me every weakness the castle. I will seize it, along with the rest of the city."

A hand touched his arm. His *wounded* arm. Pain shot through him, and Irrien spun.

The woman from before was there, reaching out as though to… what? Convince him? Prevail upon him? Irrien didn't care right then. The pain that roared through him at her touch was white hot, overwhelming all else.

"Please, my lord, what about—"

Irrien took her head from her shoulders with one sweep of his axe. He breathed hard as he waited for the pain to subside, but he knew he could not leave it at that. Tell his men that this captive had provoked him by touching his wound, and they would wonder how bad it was. They would start to wonder if there was a weakness there to exploit.

"Kill them," he ordered his men instead. "There will be plenty more captives to take, and we have no time for these."

They didn't question. Instead, they fell on the prisoners like wolves, stabbing and slashing in spite of their screams. Irrien felt no grief at it, only a faint disappointment at the waste of potential slaves. A leader did what was necessary to keep himself appearing strong.

When they stood panting in the wake of the killing, Irrien started to give commands.

"Go through the city," he commanded them. "Be ready for traps and for those who will fight back. Be thorough. I want you to sweep every street, find every straggler. Kill those who resist, take those who surrender. I want the slave lines to be long enough to stretch across the ocean."

He looked over to where the castle stood, examining it the way he might have examined the guard of a rival swordsman. His orders would slow the taking of the city, but that would give him time. Time in which to find ways into there.

He looked at the messenger Lady Stephania had sent too, standing there in obvious shock at the violence. He grabbed her by the nape of the neck, forcing her to her knees. There would be time in which to force answers from those who had them, too. He would enjoy that part of it. The weakness of others was only confirmation of his strength.

Lady Stephania was right in one way: he couldn't afford to fail against the castle's walls. He couldn't seem that weak. But he wouldn't. His men would force his way inside, and then… well, if the messenger she'd sent was anything to go by, the pickings would be rich indeed.

CHAPTER NINETEEN

Ceres woke as she always seemed to wake now, with water thrown on her, cold and dirty enough that she gasped at it. Automatically, her tongue darted out, trying to collect some of the moisture there, because in the dungeons of the castle they gave her almost nothing.

"Look at her," someone called from above her. "She's like an animal!"

"Filthy little thing," another jeered. "Dressed in scraps like that!"

It didn't seem to matter to them that it had been Stephania who had hacked her hair away; Stephania who had let her men tear Ceres's clothes until they were little more than a few bare strips of cloth. The slaves there wore more.

Ceres looked around her, and when she saw where she was, she shuddered. She was back in the training pit beneath the castle, the sand beneath her scratching as she rolled to her knees. That wasn't easy, because her hands were bound behind her at her wrists and elbows, tight enough that her shoulders ached with it.

In spite of all that they inflicted on her in the dungeons, this was the place that Ceres had come to dread. They'd taken a space that she'd once thought of as her domain, and they'd turned it into a space of humiliation. Ceres hated Stephania for that, and for so much else besides.

She sat above, of course, looking down from her throne there with an air of faint amusement. Ceres saw other nobles beside her, with servants and handmaidens. They smiled and laughed as though they were enjoying a pleasant day in the country.

Ceres hated all of them then.

Stephania signaled, and Ceres felt the nick of a blade as two guards cut her ropes. She watched them hurry back while she rubbed her wrists, and one threw something into the dirt in front of her. A sword.

Not a real one though. Not something she could hope to fight her way out of there with. This was a short, ugly, dull-looking thing with rounded edges that probably hadn't ever been sharpened. It was the kind of training blade combatlords used when they thought wood didn't give them the right feel.

In spite of it not being a real blade, Ceres snatched it up, testing the weight of it. Despite the pain and the humiliation, the world felt better when she had her hand wrapped around its grip. This was something she understood, and Stephania couldn't try to take that away from her.

She would try, though, and as a burly Empire soldier came in with his own practice blade, Ceres realized that she didn't want to do this. She didn't want to be Stephania's plaything, dancing to her tune. She threw her weapon into the sand.

"I won't fight just for your entertainment," Ceres said.

"Oh, you will," Stephania said. She gestured, and a herald blew a long note on his trumpet. "You will fight, or there will be consequences."

What consequences could there be? Dying? Right then, Ceres would rather die than be stuck suffering every day at Stephania's whim. She stood there as the guard approached, keeping her arms down as he thrust at her chest.

The sword slammed into her with bruising force, but Ceres made herself stand there without reacting. She wouldn't give Stephania the satisfaction of seeing the pain as it bruised her, or watching her stagger with the force of it.

"There," Ceres said. "I've lost. I won't fight back, Stephania!"

"Really?" Stephania countered. "Not even once you know the price?"

Ceres saw her gesture, and a young man was brought forward, his hands tied. At another signal from Stephania, a guard lifted a sword, and it was obvious that this one wasn't a training weapon.

"No," the young man begged. "No, no, please."

The guard thrust, striking the young man in almost exactly the spot Ceres's opponent had struck her. The blade slid into him and out again, leaving him to collapse while Ceres watched. She winced at that; at a life snuffed out for no better reason than because of Stephania's games.

Stephania signaled again, and more people were brought forward. Ceres thought she recognized some of the young men there, that she'd seen them before, fighting alongside the rebellion. Then she saw Sartes and she froze.

"We captured them trying to fight their way in to save you," Stephania said. "Now, you have a chance to save them, or condemn them. I am not going to kill you, but every time one of my guards lands a blow on you, one of them will suffer. You'll watch them die, and you'll realize how weak you are."

"I'll kill you," Ceres promised.

Stephania laughed. "It's not me you need to kill."

She gestured to the guard, and the man lunged at Ceres again.

Ceres barely threw herself to the side in time, coming up with the practice sword and circling. The situation wasn't fair, of course, because Stephania would never keep things even. This was a fresh, well-rested man, while her torturers hardly ever gave Ceres time to sleep. Then there was the threat hanging over her. All this man had to fear was being hit with a practice blade, while any wound on Ceres would count for the prisoners above; for her brother.

She whirled away from an attack, parried another, and then struck down across the guard's hand. She had to focus. She didn't have the strength of her Ancient One blood, but she still had the skills she'd learned in the Stade, and she could still remember the lessons the Forest People had sought to teach her. She could still remember Eoin, under a waterfall, moving with such grace that it seemed like magic.

It wasn't magic, though; it was moving as you needed to move, in harmony with the world. Ceres forced herself to relax, parrying and shifting, feeling the weight of her weapon. It didn't have an edge, but it was still iron. It still had weight and strength. It could still kill, in the right hands.

Ceres swept a strike out of the way, then chopped down, hearing the crack as she struck the soldier's knee. He started to collapse, and Ceres hit him across the jaw as he fell, sending him down into unconsciousness.

While Ceres tried to get air into her lungs, two more stepped into the training circle to take his place. They spread out, trying to encircle her, but Ceres darted between them.

"Are you just going to keep sending them until you run out of men?" Ceres called up to Stephania.

"Just until you learn your place," Stephania assured her.

One of the men cut low. Ceres stepped over the stroke, hitting him in the throat with her blunted sword. Even without an edge, it was enough to collapse him, gasping for air. She spun in time to parry another attack, barely leaned back from a third, and managed to push her attacker away.

Two more joined him as Ceres snatched up a second practice sword from one of the fallen guards.

She charged. Right then, attack was the only defense she had. She ducked as she ran in, feeling a sword whistle over her head. She struck the attacker in the stomach, but that wasn't enough to bring him down.

She parried and struck back, always moving on the edge of distance, trying to keep one of the swordsmen in between her and the others so that they couldn't strike at her all together. In spite of her efforts, she took a blow across her forearm, and heard someone scream up above. Ceres didn't dare to look up to see what was happening.

She lashed out at the hand of one of her attackers, hearing bones break as he dropped his sword. She spun past another strike, lashing out with her elbow to the base of an attacker's skull even as she parried another blow.

Somewhere in it, Ceres felt herself falling into the rhythm of the fight, feeling it the way she felt the rise and fall of her own breathing. She didn't have the speed or power that she'd possessed just a few days ago, but she could still choose the right moment to sway back from a blow, sending one man stumbling into another while she struck out to the spine with her heavy iron blade.

If this had been a fight with live blades, there would have been blood. Above, Ceres could hear some of those watching growing restless at the lack of it, but a fight didn't need blood to be deadly. There was still the crack of breaking bone, the empty gasping of men trying to drag in air through crushed throats.

Perhaps once, Ceres would have tried to hold back, but now she couldn't afford to. It wasn't just her own life on the line here, and in any case, she wasn't sure that she had the strength to do it. All she could do was flow from moment to moment, striking out without hesitation or regret whenever the moment presented itself.

She struck at joints, at bones, at the throat or the skull. She wielded her practice swords as a pair of iron clubs, there to crush and smash rather than slice or pierce. She swayed aside from a thrust, bringing a weapon down onto her enemy's elbow, then lunged in to thrust her other "sword" deep into the soft flesh of a guard's stomach. As he doubled up, she hit him behind the ear, sending him down into unconsciousness.

Ceres stood there, looking around for fresh opponents, but it seemed that those guards who weren't on the sand groaning in pain were lying there in deathly stillness. Ceres took her practice swords and plunged them into the sand, hoping that she would look stronger than she felt right then.

The truth was that she felt exhausted, as if a strong breeze might blow her over. She couldn't afford to let that show, though. She knew she had to look as though she could keep fighting all day, because otherwise Stephania would keep sending men against her.

Ceres forced herself to stare up in defiance, instead.

"Is that it?" she demanded. "Are we done? I'm sick of playing your games, Stephania. If you want to punish me for some crime only you can see, then do it, but leave the others out of this."

"You brought them into it," Stephania countered. "Would they be here if it weren't for you? All these people, and you can't save them. You'll never be enough to save them."

That hurt more than anything the others had done to her. Stephania had a knack for finding the things that poked at Ceres's heart more than anything else. She seemed to understand what would hurt most, and never hesitate to push further.

"And you still haven't learned your lesson," Stephania said. "You are not some leader. You are nothing. Allow me to demonstrate."

She clapped her hands again, and guards pushed three more figures into the ring. Three men, all with the muscles built through long training, all armed with weapons that they had long practice with. One held a sword and shield, one a trident, one a short spear. Ceres recognized the combatlords. She'd trained alongside them.

"I know I told you that we killed the combatlords," Stephania said. "But we managed to save these ones just for you. It will be just like old times, watching you fight them to the death."

Horns blew, and the three combatlords spread out around Ceres.

CHAPTER TWENTY

Sartes stood by the side of the training pit, struggling against the bonds that held him in place even though it made no difference. He couldn't just stand there. He couldn't do nothing while they were trying to break his sister like this.

Yet there was nothing he *could* do. They'd tied him to a post there, ropes around his wrists, his ankles, his throat, so that he couldn't move as much as a hand's width without the ropes tightening to half choke him. They'd put him where Ceres would be able to see him and know that she couldn't save him, but they'd been crueler than that.

They'd put him where he had to watch his fellow conscripts as they suffered. Already he'd seen Justino stabbed through the heart, had watched them hack a hand from Ullo, leaving him screaming and bleeding slowly to death. He'd heard the braying of the nobles and the guards there as they did it, laughing as if it were all some game.

What they were doing to Leyana was worse. Sartes watched her as they made her crawl through the crowd, a pitcher of wine in her hands. As the only woman with them when they'd been captured, they hadn't tied her with the others. Instead, they were treating her like the lowest of slaves. Nobles and soldiers barked commands at her. Men reached out to grab at her, making Sartes want to throw himself from the pole that held him to cut them down.

Even as he watched, a nobleman seized her by the waist, lifting Leyana up to set her on his lap. One arm held her tightly in place as she poured wine into his goblet, and when she squirmed to get away, he slapped her, hard enough that Sartes heard the crack of it. She tumbled to the floor and resumed her rounds of the others.

Sartes had no doubts about what would happen to her when they were done in the pits. Some nobleman would claim her as his own, dragging her to his bed the way they'd always done with peasants and slaves, probably beating her if she resisted. All Sartes could do was watch, and as he watched, he knew Stephania had arranged this. Only she could manage to be so cruel.

Leyana's route was taking her close to him now. Sartes tried to catch her eye to offer whatever silent support he could. Rather than pain or humiliation on her face, though, he was surprised to see a look of determination, even triumph.

She pressed close to him, and in an instant, Sartes felt something pressed into his hand. A knife.

"The noble should have been more concerned with where my hands were wandering than his," she whispered.

Sartes started to saw at the ropes.

Fear filled him as he worked at them. Leyana was still serving, still being grabbed and groped and pushed. What if something happened to her before he could finish? What if someone spotted what she'd done?

Sartes felt his hands come free, and that didn't matter anymore. As quick as thinking it, he reached up to cut the rope at his neck, then bent to get the one that held his ankles. He didn't hesitate, but instead rushed forward to where Leyana stood and grabbed her arm.

"Run!" he yelled.

The noble who was currently grabbing at her tried to hold on. Sartes stabbed him, feeling the dagger sink home, then ran. He pulled Leyana with him, sheer speed carrying him past the guards at the door. Cries behind him told him that there would quickly be pursuit.

He wished that there was time to cut the others free. To help Ceres. Instead, there was only enough time to run blindly with Leyana, picking directions almost at random through the nearly empty castle.

They sprinted, and when Sartes heard footsteps behind them, he sprinted faster.

"In here," Leyana said, pointing to a side room.

Sartes went with her, but he knew as soon as he did it that it was a mistake. The room seemed to be a storeroom, but it was almost empty, with nowhere to hide. Even as Sartes thought it, two guards followed them into the room, with swords drawn.

If Leyana hadn't been there, he might have hesitated. Instead, Sartes flung himself forward, striking at the first with the knife again and again. He shoved his opponent at the second, but that just meant they went down together, each with a hand locked on the wrist of the other's weapon arm. The guard rolled on top, his greater strength forcing his blade towards Sartes's throat.

The tip of a sword appeared from his chest as Leyana stabbed him with the first guard's sword. He seemed to freeze in place, staring down at it, then toppled sideways, away from Sartes.

Sartes stood, taking his sword.

"Are there more?" Leyana asked.

Sartes looked out of the doorway, and saw that the corridor was empty. "It seems clear for now, but we need to keep going."

"We're going to run?" Leyana asked. She sounded disappointed. "We're going to leave the others behind?"

Sartes shook his head. He could never just abandon his sister like that, or the other conscripts.

"We'll help, but we need assistance to do it. I need to find my father."

***

They walked the walls, ducking down every time they thought they saw a guard. Below, Sartes could see the city, spread out in its districts and its warrens of streets. He could see the soldiers swarming through it too, the flames there and the long chains of slaves that they were taking with them as they went from house to house. The sheer rapaciousness of it was enough to make him feel as though he wanted to run away and never look back.

He didn't, though. He kept looking. His father and the others with him had been near the castle, trying to hold the city. He just had to hope that was still the case. While he scanned the streets below, Sartes ran along to a spot where a coil of rope sat by a catapult, obviously intended to be a replacement part. If there had been anyone to man the device, it might have been difficult to take, but it seemed that those within were trusting in the strength of their walls for now.

"There!" Leyana said, pointing. "That's him, isn't it?"

Sartes looked down to a spot where small figures were fighting. He saw a burly form striking left and right with a hammer, and knew that Leyana was right. It was close enough to the walls that Sartes decided to risk calling out.

"Father!" he yelled. He started to wave. "Father!"

"Careful," Leyana said. "You'll attract the guards."

That was the danger. Even though there were far fewer people than there had been in the castle, there were still *some* guards out there. Sartes could keep waving, though, and soon, the small figure of his father turned to look at him. Sartes saw him and a couple of other figures break away from the skirmish, running for the castle walls.

While his father ran closer, Sartes looked for a place to anchor the rope he held. He ended up tying it around the unused catapult's frame, hoping that the great weight of it would be enough.

He dropped the rope over the wall and waited. There was so much that could go wrong now. What if someone saw them? What if his father fell?

"It will be all right," Leyana assured him, but right then, all Sartes could feel was the tension running through the moment.

He saw his father pulling himself over the wall and reached down to pull him up. Two smiths followed, strong men, but obviously ones who had been in a lot of fights today. One had bruises all over his face. The other had a bloody bandage wrapped around his shoulder.

His father pulled him into a tight embrace. "Sartes, you're alive! When you didn't come back, I was so worried. What happened?"

Sartes didn't know how to put it. "We were ambushed. Ceres… they're making her fight in a pit. I couldn't get her out alone."

"I have no doubt you did everything you could," his father said.

Sartes wished that he could be so sure. Maybe he could have stayed and fought. Maybe he could have been more careful in the tunnels.

"And you're free," his father said. Sartes saw him swallow. "That's good. There isn't much time. They're in the city now."

Sartes nodded. He could see the invaders from the wall. They formed a ring he couldn't see a way through; a noose tightening on the castle.

"We can't run yet," Sartes said. "We still need to get Ceres out."

His father looked at him. "You have an idea, don't you?"

Sartes nodded. He'd been thinking about this since they captured him. They'd blocked off so many of the ways out, but what was blocked could be unblocked, couldn't it?

"We find one of the entrances they think are secure, and we open it," Sartes said. "They won't have people on it, because they don't have enough to watch them all. We couldn't force our way in from outside, but now that we're *inside*… we can let the rebellion in."

It was a simple plan, but it felt like a good one. Stephania had only taken the castle because she'd been able to shut the rebels out. If they could provide a way back in…

Sartes saw his father shake his head.

"It's too late for that," he said. "An hour ago, two hours, and it might have been possible. Now… there isn't enough of the rebellion left here, Sartes. We tried to hold back the invaders, and they just washed over us."

For a moment, Sartes stood there, feeling broken. It had seemed so simple. Now, there was nothing. He looked out at the dark line of Felldust's army. He knew his father was right. That would be here soon. Even if they could somehow take the castle, how long could they hold? If they tried to sneak out, they would be caught, because it was obvious they were being thorough in sacking the city. If they tried to fight, they would just be overwhelmed.

What did that leave?

The answer came to Sartes slowly, and it seemed insane as he thought of it, but what other options were there? What was there that might work?

"Then we let the invaders into the castle," he said.

The others looked at him as though he'd just proposed that they should jump from the walls.

"What?" Leyana asked. "Sartes, that would mean chaos."

Sartes nodded. "And chaos is what we need right now. If we stay here with things as they are, eventually Stephania kills us. If we go out there, Felldust's army kills us. If we let them in, maybe they're all so busy killing one another that we can escape."

It was a desperate plan, Sartes knew that. There were so many ways it could go wrong. He might be bringing their deaths down on them, but wasn't even that better than some of the things Stephania might do?

"We have to do this," he said. "Father, will you do it? Will you find a gate to open?"

His father hesitated, and Sartes couldn't blame him. What he was asking would bring violence to the castle that otherwise wouldn't touch it. It would cost people their lives.

"All right," his father said at last. "What will you do while I open the gate?"

Sartes nodded in the direction of the main body of the castle. There was only one thing he could do.

"I'm going to go get Ceres."

***

Berin crept down through the castle courtyard, weighing his hammer in his hand. It was almost as heavy as his thoughts right then. What he was about to do would bring death to a lot of people.

"Are we really going to do this?" Caspar asked. He'd been one of Berin's smiths only a couple of weeks, but he was a good man in a fight. J'ket, beside him, was a former slave who'd been a smith back in the Southlands.

"First we need to find a gate we can open," Berin said. It wasn't an answer, but right then, he didn't *have* an answer. He

107

could imagine the slaughter when Felldust's army broke into the castle, the rapes, the looting.

He didn't have to imagine it, because he'd already seen it in the rest of the city.

"There," J'ket said. "They've welded it shut, but these imperials can't weld worth my hammer scale."

It turned out that he had a good eye for it, because one look at the small gate he was pointing to told Berin that it was the one that they wanted. The guards had indeed tried to weld metal bars in place over it, but Berin could see the bad welds there. Only the original bolts would be strong, and they would be easy enough to pull back. Even the couple of wooden bars nailed in place would be easy to rip clear.

"This is the one," Berin agreed.

He started to hammer at the bad welds, the sound of metal on metal ringing out around the courtyard. They were stronger than they looked, and for a moment, he thought maybe he'd picked the wrong gate. The first one gave.

Just as it did, a group of guards approached. There were half a dozen of them. Too many to win against, but right then, that wasn't the point.

"Hold them off," Berin said, pointing with his hammer. "I need to get this door open."

They didn't hesitate, and Berin was proud of them for that. They took up a position in front of him, swinging their hammers to keep the soldiers back. Berin swung his own, but at the door welds, not at their attackers. He hit with all the force he'd built in years of blade-smithing, striking right at the point of the weakest welds.

He dared a glance back at the battle. Caspar was grappling with one of the guards while another was down. J'ket was giving ground, a fresh wound open on his side. Berin saw him charge, but couldn't watch the rest. He had to focus on the doors.

He struck, shattering welds even while the sounds of battle continued behind him. He broke apart metal, ripped free chains, and tore at wood.

When he looked back again, Caspar and J'ket were on the ground, while two of the soldiers remained standing. J'ket was still moving, trying to keep his hammer between him and the enemy, while Caspar had all the stillness of the grave.

Berin's hand closed over the last bolt. If he pulled this, the gate would be open. The invaders would have a way in. He would be responsible for whatever followed. He found himself thinking of the nobles in the castle, the servants, the soldiers.

The same people who were tormenting his daughter even then.
"If you've any sense, you'll run, lads," he said.
He pulled back the bolt and threw the door open.

CHAPTER TWENTY ONE

Ceres stood there watching as her brother made his break for freedom. She felt relief in that moment, and something more. She felt triumph. It was a small victory over Stephania, and there was at least one more that she could gain.

She threw down her blunted excuses for swords, turning her back on the combatlords Stephania had sent into the training pit. "I'm not going to play your games anymore, Stephania. I won't fight for your amusement."

She heard the crowd of nobles boo then, as if this were really the Stade. As if she were being a coward by not taking part.

"Then your rebels will die with every strike the combatlords land," Stephania said. She gestured to the waiting combatlords, and Ceres braced herself for the strikes they would land.

They didn't move.

"Fight her!" Stephania ordered. "Fight her, or die."

"We'd rather die," one of them said, folding his arms. "I'm sick of playing nobles' games."

Ceres could see the fury on Stephania's face then. She'd never liked things being out of her control. This had to be impossible for her.

"Then die," Stephania snapped. "Guards! Kill the combatlords!"

They poured down into the small training space, and Ceres snatched up her weapons again. She stood with her back to the combatlords, waiting.

The soldiers charged.

Their weapons were sharp this time, but Ceres didn't care. If anything, it made it easier, because now she could afford to take a scratch from one without a prisoner losing an arm.

She dove into the fight, striking out with her blunted weapons. As soon as she knocked down a soldier, she snatched up his sword, trading it for one of the practice weapons they'd foisted on her. She thrust it through another guard, snatched his sword too, and spun to strike at the next.

The combatlords seemed to have the same idea, casting aside the training weapons Stephania had allowed them in favor of snatching blades from their attackers. They spun and cut now, working in formation with Ceres, and even though she didn't have the strength she'd once had, they had more than enough to make up for it. She saw one pick up a soldier and throw him into another, while a second barged a soldier straight into the wall of the training pit, stabbing as he closed in.

She parried an attack, dropped to cut at the leg of one of the soldiers, then bounced up, her second blade sweeping across his throat. Before, she'd been a thing of crushing violence, using the weight of the heavy practice blades to attack. Now, she moved them like razor-edged clouds, using their speed and sharpness to make up for the leaden exhaustion seeping into her limbs.

That was far too real after so much fighting, but Ceres didn't care. She parried and thrust, ducked and cut, forcing herself to keep moving on the shifting sand. She stumbled slightly, recovered, and cut a soldier's head from his shoulders.

Quickly, the soldiers pulled back, obviously unwilling to keep risking their lives against such trained killers.

"Enough," Stephania said from above. "We'll try this another way. Bows!"

Some of the guards above stepped forward, drawn bows in their hands.

"You have a choice," Stephania said. "You can fight Ceres, or you can die. And you, Ceres, if you won't fight, I'll have them put arrows in your legs. You can still crawl to the First Stone that way when I give you to him."

The guards with the bows didn't waver in their aim. Ceres wondered if she could dodge the arrows somehow, or maybe put herself between them and the combatlords. She was the reason they were in this situation, after all. She stepped in their way, but the guards were all around the pit. There was no way for them to dodge.

That was when the horns started to sound. They blared loud enough that they seemed to fill the world, and shouts came with them, as well as screams.

A guard came running in. "Invaders! Invaders are in the building! The gates have fallen!"

He shouted it as a warning, but he didn't do it quickly enough. A figure in dark strips of cloth came up behind him, thrusting a blade through him. Guards turned to fight, cutting down the first of the invaders, but there were more, and more after that.

The guards who had been pointing bows were fighting the Felldust soldiers now. Ceres stood there as above, nobles started to scream, servants ran, and Stephania stood, trying to shout orders.

In spite of the chaos, she smiled to see Stephania like that.

"So much for being in control," she said.

***

111

Stephania stood on her throne, trying to shout orders to her men, trying to push down the panic that threatened to overwhelm her.

"Fight back!" she ordered. "You, why are you running? We have to hold them!"

She watched as Felldust soldiers forced their way into the room. She saw a servant get in the way, only to be cut down by the stroke of a curved knife. A soldier struggled with one of the invaders, trying to push him back even as another stabbed him from the side.

Stephania could feel the panic in the room. Nobles scrambled over one another to try to find an exit. Men who'd boasted about their fighting prowess pushed and shoved to run away. Women screamed as the attackers grabbed for them.

Stephania felt a scream rising in her own throat and pushed it down. She would stay calm. She would stay in control.

"What are we going to do?" a girl demanded, grabbing at Stephania's hands. "Help us, your majesty!"

Stephania recognized her as the girl who was supposed to be her double, but right then, the two didn't look much alike, despite wearing the same dress. This was just a panicking little girl, while Stephania was in control. She was—

A warrior in dust-ingrained armor came at her, a wavy bladed axe raised to strike. On instinct, Stephania shoved the girl into his path as the axe swept down. Her shriek was cut short as the axe plunged into her, cutting through her from collar bone to abdomen. Stephania stepped back, letting others do the work of fighting.

Some of them were trying. The guards were struggling to bring their swords into play, stabbing and slashing despite the confines of the crowd. If they'd been fighting on the walls, they might have had a chance, but with the invaders inside the castle, this was a last stand rather than an organized defense.

Some of the noblemen seemed to realize that there was no way out except through the attackers. They drew their short, mostly ceremonial, weapons, and started to fight back. Stephania saw one fall with his throat cut open, saw a noblewoman pushed down into the fighting pit.

A hand closed over her arm and Stephania spun, going for one of her hidden blades. She breathed a sigh of relief when she saw Elethe there, a bloody knife in one hand and a determined expression on her face.

"This way, your majesty," she said, pulling Stephania down toward the training pit's entrance. One of Felldust's men stepped in their way and Elethe stabbed him with the speed of a striking snake. "We need to get you out of here."

"This is my *castle*," Stephania argued automatically.

"And it's full of invaders," Elethe snapped back. She seemed to remember herself. "I'm sorry, my lady, but… we have to keep you safe."

Stephania nodded. "You're right. We need to go. The rest doesn't matter."

She'd been prepared to abandon all of it just a short while ago, after all. She'd traveled to Felldust with almost nothing. She still had her poisons and her emergency jewels. Even as a queen, she carried those with her.

Elethe led the way through the violence, guiding her way through it the way a fish might have slipped through a shoal. A warrior moved into her way and she stabbed again. Stephania shoved back a noblewoman who grabbed hold of her, begging for help.

They made it to the entrance the slaves used when they trained, slipping through it, down into the sweat stink of the space beyond. It was dark there, but Stephania was used to sneaking through the dark. Elethe led the way, snatching a torch from the wall and lighting it, but Stephania followed close behind. She drew a short blade, ready for trouble.

"Do you know which tunnels are blocked?" Stephania asked.

"It's hard to tell for sure," Elethe replied. "There might be invaders down here. We'll find the way."

Stephania had no doubt that they would. They set off through the near dark, and at every step, Stephania had the feeling that someone was watching. That someone was following them through the dark, stalking the way a hunter might track an animal. Stephania dismissed that as just her fear talking.

She spotted a turning she thought she recognized, and set off again.

"This way."

She led the way down through the tunnels now, only pausing when she saw figures ahead. She heard them talking and recognized the words in the tongue of Felldust.

"…told us to wait here and cut off escape. Wait, is that a light?"

Elethe edged forward. "What do you want me to do, my lady?"

Stephania pushed her without thinking, sending her stumbling into the path of the soldiers while she stood back and watched. Yes, Elethe had saved her life, but Stephania had to be practical about these things. Either Elethe would do well, or she would be the distraction Stephania needed to escape.

She watched the guards draw their weapons, then smiled as Elethe leapt forward to the attack. Her knife rose and fell as she struck at the first of them. The second moved in behind her, and that was when Stephania stepped in with her own blade. She cut the warrior's throat and let him fall while Elethe stared up at her.

"You pushed me straight at them," she complained.

Stephania gave her an even look. "I did what I thought was best to take them by surprise. There was no time to give you a warning." She reached out to touch Elethe's shoulder. "You did well. I won't forget."

Stephania wasn't sure if she would believe it, but it didn't really matter. Her handmaiden had already shown that she was loyal. She would do what Stephania required.

"This way," Stephania said, leading the way through the tunnels. She knew them. She'd made it her business to know them. She took a small key from a collection at her belt, unlocking a gate. She kept going.

As she walked, she tried not to think about everything she'd just lost. She'd gambled on holding out in the castle, forcing the First Stone to talk, and building her power base as he withdrew. She'd even considered seducing him, and becoming the queen of a combined empire that would stretch across the sea.

That was done now. Her bargaining chips were gone. Even now, Felldust's troops were cutting down her nobles, taking her valuables.

"Someone betrayed us, Elethe," Stephania said. "Someone opened a gate. Who would betray *me*?"

"I don't know, my lady," Elethe said, although she didn't sound certain about it. Stephania ignored that.

"We will rebuild, though. We will use the tunnels to get beyond the city walls, and then get clear. I have some valuables with me, and I know where there are caches. Even if we can't retake Delos, I will set up somewhere else."

There would always be room for a noble and a spinner of secrets. Stephania might even go to Felldust, and start to take the city over one piece of information at a time. She still had her networks. She still had her mind.

Ahead, Stephania thought she saw a glimmer of light. If she remembered this tunnel correctly, it would bring her out in a small grove beyond the walls. Hopefully, it would be beyond the lines of Felldust's army too. From there, she could slip away, steal a horse, find a ship. She would sell Elethe to slavers if she had to, although it would be better to have her protection. Perhaps it would be better to keep her loyal with more half-promises and suggestions. Whatever it took to stay safe.

She was almost out into the light when a figure shuffled out in front of them. For a moment, Stephania thought that it had to be another straggler from Felldust's army, silhouetted against the light. A woman this time, not that it made any difference. Then she saw the woman's face, and froze.

"Well, princess," Felene said as she stepped out with a grim smile. "Fancy meeting you here."

CHAPTER TWENTY TWO

Felene leaned against the wall as nonchalantly as she could. She definitely didn't want to let Stephania know that it was the only thing holding her up right then.

"Surprised to see me?" Felene asked, forcing herself to smile. "You shouldn't be. What did you *think* was going to happen when you tried to kill me?"

"Mostly," Stephania said, "I thought that you would have the decency to die."

Felene's smile widened at that. "Ah, that's where you went wrong, thinking that I have any decency. If you'd waited a while longer before betraying me, maybe we'd have had a chance to find out."

Stephania made a face at that. "In your dreams, thief."

Ordinarily, Felene would have made a quip about all the things Stephania might have been doing in her dreams, but the truth was that the only dreams she'd had when it came to Stephania had her dying. Dying a hundred different ways for what she'd done, and none of them seemed like enough.

Felene saw Elethe there behind her mistress. The dreams involving her had been more complicated, but Felene pushed them out of her mind. It wasn't as though there was some bright future waiting for her after this.

It had been hard enough to get to this point. She'd slipped in through the attacking fleet. She'd found a point near the castle from which to watch. She'd even resumed her disguise as one of the Felldust troops for a while as she made her way from building to building. All the while, she'd tried to ignore the pain of her wound, and the coughing that seemed to bring more drops of blood each time.

When she'd seen the gate open, the temptation had been to pour in with the rest of them, but Felene had held back. She'd known she wouldn't get what she wanted by going along with the others. She'd known that Stephania would be quick to run from the castle the moment it fell.

She'd gone down into the tunnels beneath the city, finding her way by feel and the dim light of a thief's lamp. There had been guards down there, and more of the soldiers of Felldust, but Felene had learned to hide on the Isle of Prisoners, where the hunters had been far more dangerous than any soldiers.

She'd walked until she'd spotted Stephania, then she'd stalked her through the dark, waiting for her moment. Now it was here. Felene drew a long knife.

"Felene?" Elethe said, hurrying forward. "You're alive?"

She threw her arms around Felene, and for a moment, Felene could almost believe that she meant it. That she was sorry for her part in trying to kill Felene. That she actually cared. She certainly *sounded* as though she was happy to see her again.

But then, she'd seemed happy on the boat, too.

Elethe moved back with her hands on Felene's shoulders, standing there as if waiting for Felene to kiss her. As if waiting for the courage to do it herself.

Felene heard Elethe gasp as the blade she held slid home. Up under the ribs, straight into the heart. Felene saw her mouth form itself into a small O of surprise, as if she'd expected this to go differently.

"Did you think I'd fall for the same thing again?" Felene demanded, her anger welling over as she struck. "Did you think you could fool me?"

"But I wasn't trying to—" Elethe began. She didn't manage to finish it. Felene felt her shudder as the life went out of her, held up only because Felene still had hands on her.

She held Elethe there a moment or two longer. It was the closest the two of them had been, but not half as close as Felene had briefly hoped they could be.

Grief threatened to well up in Felene then. She pushed it down while she pulled the knife out and let her collapse. It was done. There was no going back. Dwelling on what Elethe might or might not have been about to say would cause her nothing but pain, and Felene already had more than enough of that.

Stephania didn't seem to agree, of course.

"It seems I owe you my thanks," she said. "I should have spotted that my handmaiden's loyalties were still… divided."

"Is that all you have to say?" Felene asked. "She served you. She *chose* you, and you feel nothing about her dying?"

She watched Stephania shrug.

"Should I get emotional about the death of a servant? Besides, you're the one who killed her."

That was true, and Felene suspected that she would regret it for the brief remainder of her life. Regret seemed to be something she specialized in these days.

"It hurts, doesn't it?" Stephania said. "Have you considered simply dying the way you should?"

She flung something then, and Felene barely leaned back out of the way in time. Needles skittered off the wall of the tunnel.

"You'll have to do a lot better than that," Felene said. "And I'm pretty sure you can't, princess. You can't actually *fight,* can you? Just attack when someone isn't looking and hope for the best."

Sure enough, Stephania flung herself forward, a knife in her hand. Felene stepped out of the way, sent her stumbling, and kicked the blade from her fingers as she fell.

"I have a lot of regrets in my life," Felene said, hefting her own weapon. "But you know what? Killing you isn't going to be one of them."

***

Athena crept through the slums of Delos, a stolen blanket wrapped around her like a cloak. The fear of a hunted animal wormed through her with every step, and every sound sent her skittering into the cover beneath walls.

She was hungry. In the time since Stephania had ejected her from the castle, she hadn't found anything to eat. She'd been forced to drink rain water taken from a water butt, and she'd only found shelter to sleep in because so many people had abandoned the city.

Her city.

How had it come to this? Not long ago, she had been powerful beyond dreams. She had been the queen of the Empire, her husband long reigning and strong. Now Claudius was dead. Her son was gone. The Empire had fallen both to the rebellion and the invaders.

Athena pressed herself back into the space between two walls while a group of warriors in the dust-colored clothes of Felldust went past, chasing after a small group of commoners. Athena watched as they cut down almost all the men, taking the women and some of the younger boys in chains. They stood over one of the older women as if assessing her, then cut her throat as if it was nothing.

She found herself wondering what would happen if they caught her. Would they kill her out of hand? Would they take her as a slave? What would happen if she announced who she was? Would that make them more or less likely to kill her? Would it make them kill her quicker or slower?

"Better not to be caught," Athena whispered to herself.

She needed to get out of the city, but the truth was that she didn't know how. She'd prided herself on being the one who could deal with the intrigues of the court to get things done, but she wasn't in the castle anymore. She didn't have soldiers to help her, or wealth, or anything beyond the clothes she stood up in.

A part of her wanted to go out and announce herself to the soldiers then, just to get it over with. It was better than stumbling around the streets, not knowing what to do. Maybe they wouldn't decide she was too old to enslave. Maybe they would take her if she announced that she was the former queen.

Former queen. Athena had never imagined herself as that. She had assumed that she would be the queen in some form for the rest of her life, either ruling alongside her husband, or controlling the Empire through her son. Now, she had neither.

She wasn't used to changing her ways of thinking. The world ran the way it did because of channels of power that had been carved and re-carved through the world. Status, propriety, all of it built up into something that made the world something she could work with. Now, she was having to think of ways to get out of a city she no longer had any control over, able only to hide, with no one to turn to for help.

She certainly wasn't going to trust any of the city's people. After all that had happened, they would probably kill her as quickly as help her. She'd thought that enough cruelty could keep them in their place. Instead, it had just poisoned them against her.

If only Claudius could ride up and take me away from this, Athena thought, creeping out of her hiding place and continuing on her route through the city.

He'd been the kind of man to do that once. He'd been the errant knight, and she the fair young maiden. It was strange how time and politics changed things. She'd never really wanted to marry Claudius. He'd just been a route to power. He'd been a duty to fulfill, along with so many others. Maybe that was a part of what had gone wrong. Maybe if she'd thought a little less about duty…

"Never look back," she told herself. "Always look forward."

That was hard to do, though, when there was so much more of her life behind her than ahead. Still, she needed to focus on the things that would keep her alive. She knew there would be no chance of getting past the walls with the invaders encircling them. Her only hope now was the docks.

She started to walk down in the direction of them.

Again and again, she had to duck back into the shadows, hiding from the soldiers who worked their way through the city. Athena had assumed that the fall of a city would look more chaotic than this. She'd assumed that the streets would be full of marauding enemies, with no order to the violence. Instead, they seemed to be moving systematically from house to house, pulling people out into the street, killing some, chaining others. Anyone who fought back died.

Avoiding that was hard. Athena found herself squeezing between houses, ducking under overhangs and hiding in shrubbery. Only the fact that she was heading for the docks helped her. The invaders seemed to assume that those fleeing would head deeper into the city, or make for the walls.

Eventually, Athena caught sight of the docks. That was enough that she almost collapsed with it, because the invading fleet filled the harbor, taking up almost all the available space.

There was nowhere to go. There was no way to escape. Athena sat there, and for the first time since Stephania had ejected her, she sobbed. She sat there, waiting for the moment when some invader would come and lock chains about her wrists, not caring anymore.

That was when she saw the second fleet approaching from beyond the harbor. At first, it seemed like just one more addition to the Felldust fleet. One more set of sharks there to pick at the carcass of the city. Only one thing kept Athena watching.

There was an imperial galley at the heart of it.

That was enough to make her stand, continuing on her route down to the docks. Perhaps all hope wasn't gone after all.

CHAPTER TWENTY THREE

Ceres fought, and now it felt as though she'd been fighting forever. From the first moments she'd fallen into the Stade, from the moment she'd started serving Thanos as his weapons bearer, she'd been fighting, and this felt like the culmination of it.

Guards came at her, and warriors from Felldust. They charged, they snarled, they cut and they thrust. It didn't make any difference. Ceres whirled out of the way, parried and cut, keeping herself in the space where she could flow in the moment. She felt a sword slice across her forearm, a spear tip puncture the skin above her hip. None of it made any difference.

In that moment, she *was* the battle. She was one piece of it and the whole of it, the way a droplet of water couldn't be separated from the rest of the ocean. She followed the tide of the battle, ducking under the stroke of a wide-bladed sword, thrusting up in its wake.

The combatlords stayed with her, and in a battle this closely pressed, Ceres found herself grateful for that. It almost didn't matter how good she was with a sword when an attack could come from anywhere. If she couldn't see it, couldn't anticipate it, then even the skills Eoin's people had taught her couldn't help. With the combatlords at her back, she could trust that they would stop the blows that would kill her otherwise.

Ceres fought, and while she did, she heard the screams of the nobles, the cries of the servants. Ceres shook her head. She couldn't do anything to help them. Even if she could have, they'd stood by and watched her torment. Many of them had yelled their approval while she'd been beaten. While the conscripts had been murdered.

They would have to save themselves, if they could.

Even as she thought it, Ceres saw that Stephania was making her own efforts. She and one of her handmaidens leapt down into the fighting pit, and from there ran for the gate that allowed slaves into it.

Ceres started after her, but there were soldiers in the way. She wanted to scream at them then, to yell at them to get out of her way. Following Stephania was as instinctive as breathing right then, but the way the battle ran was wrong for it, and Ceres couldn't break free from the wash of it without opening herself up to more attacks.

She pressed forward, trying to cut her way through the problem, but there were too many enemies for that. Where the guards and the invaders had allies and clear enemies, for Ceres, it seemed that everyone was a foe.

That could be an advantage, though, and Ceres threw herself into the middle of it, cutting left and right. She took the blow of a hammer on her crossed blades, hacked at the arm of its holder, and turned in time to sweep aside a fighting pick.

She turned, looking for her next opponent, and in that moment she saw her father and her brother joining the battle. They were up above, where the conscripts were still tied to their posts. She saw Sartes cut through the ropes of one boy, while her father and a girl Ceres didn't know tried to protect against those pressing in.

They kept going, even though it was too late for many of the conscripts. Ceres saw one of Felldust's warriors thrust a blade into one of the tied boys, while a noble cut the throat of another. Ceres wished then that she could leap up there to help, but all she could do was plunge back into the fight in the pit and hope it would be enough.

She started to cut a path to her brother and father. Beside her, the combatlords pushed men back, smashed them from their feet, cut them down. There seemed to be fewer soldiers attacking them now, as if realizing that their efforts needed to be on the foes who had come into the castle.

"Down here!" she called up, and saw her brother look down. She watched him nod, then lower the girl with him into the fighting pit. She had a sword, and she looked determined to Ceres.

"This is Leyana," Sartes said. "Look after her."

One look at Sartes's expression when he passed her down told Ceres everything she needed to know about the two of them.

The conscript followed, then her father. Sartes was last, hopping down lightly onto the sand. One of the Felldust warriors ran at him as he rolled to his feet, but Ceres ran in to cut the man's spear in half. She opened his throat with the backswing, turning to her brother and pointing.

"That way!" she yelled over the noise of the battle. "Through the slave entrance, to the tunnels."

There were enough of them now to push their way through the battle as a wedge. Ceres formed its tip, cutting down anyone who was foolish enough to try to slow them. Two of the three combatlords flanked her, providing strength and pushing power to break through the walls of men in front of them. Sartes, Leyana, her father, and the conscript came next. The final combatlord brought up the rear, so that no one could ambush them from behind.

They pushed forward, heading for the spot where the pit gave way to the tunnels. Chasing after Stephania, because Ceres wasn't going to let her get away after everything she'd done.

They pushed through the last few, and then plunged down into the tunnels. Sartes had a light, and so he had to go first, but Ceres followed as close as she could. She thought she could see the flicker of another light far ahead, and followed behind it.

Twists and turns followed, down beneath the earth, and Ceres let Sartes guide her, although she kept her eye on the flicker of light as well.

Perhaps that was why the warriors who smashed into them took her by surprise. One barreled into her, taking Ceres from her feet. The other smashed past her, and she heard her father grunt as a blade grazed him.

She rolled with the man who'd slammed into her, coming up on top and grabbing for his wrist in the near dark. She forced it away from her even as he grabbed her wrist in return. That was bad, because it turned this into a contest of strength, and although she was on top, she could feel that the man beneath her was stronger.

She snapped her head forward, smashing her forehead into her attacker's nose once and then again. It gave her the opening she needed to wrench her sword arm free, thrusting down and feeling her blade slide into his throat. The man she was grappling with made a small, swift sound of pain, and then it was done.

Ceres spun, ready to help with the second man, but the others had already rushed in to fight him, and he was down. Her father was rubbing his shoulder, but Ceres felt a surge of relief that he was all right. She'd been so worried that she might turn around to find him gone.

"They're in the tunnels," Sartes said.

Ceres could hear the fear there. "We'll find a way through. They won't catch us."

But they would catch Stephania. Ceres was going to find her, and she was going to kill her. She was going to end this.

If she could find her.

"Which way?" Ceres asked. "Which way would Stephania have gone?"

She watched while her brother thought for a moment.

"She'd have keys to some of the tunnels she closed off," Sartes said, "so the quickest way for her to get out would be… that way."

Ceres didn't hesitate. She set off through the dimness of the tunnels, moving as fast as she dared. Her feet caught rocks as she ran, but she managed to recover her footing each time, forcing herself to keep going. She had to believe that Stephania couldn't move this fast, even if she had a head start.

At each crossroads, she paused, looking around for signs, waiting for Sartes to catch up with the others. Sartes had spent more time than she had in the tunnels under the city, working there with Anka and learning the routes. Ceres had no idea where they were by now, but Sartes seemed certain each time.

"We're somewhere under the cattle market," he said. "Can't you smell it?"

Ceres could, but she hadn't thought to use it as a directional marker. More importantly, she had other things to focus on right then.

"Which way?" she asked.

Sartes pointed. "She'll be trying to get to the docks. That way."

Ceres ran on. She could hear other sounds down in the tunnels now. She could hear booted feet and calls in a language she didn't understand. She guessed that it was only a matter of time before the tunnels filled with Felldust soldiers, hunting for the last people hiding from them.

Ceres didn't want to have to fight a whole army. She doubted that she could come close to it now, with only human strength and no powers to turn her enemies to stone. Ceres found herself missing that for a moment. If there was one person who deserved to be turned into a statue, it was Stephania. She could stand there, beautiful but harmless, for the rest of time.

That wasn't an option, though, so she was going to have to do things the other way.

"Ceres," her father said. "Wait."

Ceres paused, but she couldn't stay patient. She shifted in place, looking ahead in the hope that she might catch a glimpse of her quarry.

"There's no time to wait," she said. "Every second I hesitate is a second in which Stephania might get away."

"So let her get away," his father said. "It's done. Stephania doesn't have the Empire's army to command. She doesn't have any power. She's just running now. She isn't a threat."

Ceres shook her head. Her father didn't understand what Stephania was like. Not the way she did.

"Stephania will always be a threat. You could abandon her on an island somewhere, surrounded by nothing but birds and trees, and she would find a way to make them into her spies."

"I know she hurt you," her father said, putting a hand on her arm.

"She did," Ceres said. "And she hurt Sartes, and who knows how many other people? She won't stop unless someone stops her. Permanently."

"Is it worth your life?" her father countered. "You can hear them, in the tunnels. I don't want to lose my daughter."

Ceres shook her head. "It won't come to that. Which way, Sartes?"

She saw her brother hesitate, then point. He obviously understood. "Stephania will be going that way," he said. He pointed in a different direction. "But Ceres, I think we should go *that* way. It will take us to one of the rebellion's alternate exits. We can get to a boat. Father's right. The Empire is done. Stephania is done. There won't be much time before this place is full of Felldust soldiers."

Ceres saw him look over to Leyana. It was only natural that he wanted to protect her. Ceres knew what she had to do.

"You go," she said. "Get down to the water and see if you can find us a boat. I'll catch up."

"Ceres—" her father began.

"I'll catch up," Ceres promised again, and she started to run.

Stephania wasn't going to get away this time.

CHAPTER TWENTY FOUR

From the deck of the smuggling ship, Thanos watched the Bone Folk slam into the back of Felldust's fleet. It was a moment that was simultaneously impressive and terrifying, the wood and bone ships ripping into their targets, the warriors starting to swarm over the decks of their foes.

It looked incredible, unstoppable, destructive beyond words. Thanos saw warriors cutting down their foes with brutal strength, saw Jeva leap and cut a man's head from his shoulders, saw a dozen more moments that proved just what deadly warriors the Bone Folk were.

Thanos knew it wouldn't be enough. It could never be enough.

Their fleet had looked so impressive when it had been traveling, and individually, the warriors of Jeva's people were far more dangerous than the masses of Felldust's horde, but against the might of the invasion fleet, they were too few. At best, they could be a distraction. The fact that they were willing to die to be that little made Thanos's heart clench.

They were willing to do it for Ceres. Thanos could understand that part.

"This is as close as we can get," the captain of the smuggling ship said as Thanos clambered into a small skiff. "From this point, you're on your own. I'll probably make my way further up the coast, but I can't wait this time. You understand?"

Thanos understood. It would be suicide for the man to wait with his crew by the harbor. More than that, it sounded as though he didn't expect Thanos to come back at all. Thanos didn't mind that. The captain had already done more than Thanos could have hoped for.

He sat while they lowered the skiff into the water, then hurried it forward using oars. The surrounding ships would have blocked the wind if he'd tried the small sail, so he pulled his way through the violence and the chaos of it.

It was terrifying, rowing his way through a battle. Screams and voices yelling orders filled the air. Arrows struck the water like flying fish returning to their homes. Thanos watched as a Bone Folk ship with a great ram struck one of the Felldust barges in what seemed like slow motion, timbers broader than Thanos was tall snapping as though they were nothing.

If this hadn't been for Ceres, Thanos wouldn't have risked something as mad as this.

A jar of flaming oil struck the water ahead, burning in a film on top of the low waves. Thanos rowed back as hard as he could, trying to avoid it. His small boat could never survive something like that, and in the heart of a battle, he had no doubt that predators waited in the harbor waters if he fell in.

He rowed as hard as he could for shore, not aiming for the main jetties of the harbor, but instead for a patch of shingle nearby where small fishing boats stood untouched, obviously abandoned by their owners when they realized that the oncoming fleet would block their escape.

That made Thanos wonder how long his own escape route would last. How long would the Bone Folk be able to fight? How long would they be able to keep a route through Felldust's fleet open? How many of them would die doing it?

Thanos didn't know, but right then, it didn't matter. He had to find Ceres.

He pulled the boat up onto the shale, drawing his longsword as he stepped down. He had no doubt that it would be a fight if anyone saw him, and there was a long route between him and the castle. He would find Ceres there and he would get her out of the city, whatever it took.

He ran up through the city. He saw men fighting there, sacking houses one by one. Thanos gripped his blade tighter. A part of him wanted to run to those houses, fight the attackers off, and save those within.

"You're dead if you do it, Thanos," a familiar voice said. A woman's voice. "Oh, I know you want to help, but there are too many, and after all, they're only peasants."

A woman stepped from between two buildings, holding out a hand. Thanos half raised his weapon, expecting an attack, but it was obvious that she was alone. She was dirty and starved looking, with rings around her eyes that suggested she hadn't slept, and a blanket wrapped roughly about her shoulders.

Thanos wasn't sure that he would have recognized Queen Athena if she hadn't spoken.

"Quick, this way," she said, gesturing for him to follow her back into the house. "They've been past this spot, so they won't be back for a while. One of the advantages of systematic plunder is that you know where you're safe."

"I would have expected you to be perfectly safe in the castle," Thanos said, but he followed her. The queen was right: he needed to get out of sight.

They ducked back into a house together. The door wasn't locked. If anything, it looked as though it had been broken open with an axe. Thanos didn't want to think about what had happened to the inhabitants.

It gave Thanos a moment to decide what he felt about this meeting, but he wasn't sure that it was enough. The last time he'd seen Athena, she'd been falsely condemning him for the murder of her husband, in order to save her son. She was a viper, yet now she seemed less like an enemy and more like just an older woman caught up in the violence.

"What are you doing out here?" Thanos asked. "I thought Ceres had you imprisoned."

He watched while Athena sat down on a rough wooden chair that was practically all that remained of the furniture there.

"When Stephania took the castle from her, she decided I wasn't worth keeping around. It seems both the women in your life hate me, Thanos."

They probably had every reason to, but Thanos didn't say that.

"And Ceres?" he asked.

"Was Stephania's to torment, the last I saw," Athena answered. She seemed neither pleased nor displeased by that, where once she might have reveled in it. "Alive, though, if that's what you're asking."

Was that what this was? Was the former queen there to hurt him? Perhaps she planned to demand his help. If so, she would be waiting a long time after all she had done.

"You're wondering what I'm doing here," she guessed. "What I want from you."

Thanos nodded.

"Frankly, I'm waiting for assassins to jump out of the woodwork. You were trying to kill me the last time we saw one another."

He tried to summon more sympathy for her, and he did have some, the same way he would have sympathy for anyone caught up in this situation. This was a woman who could have been like a mother to him.

The truth was that she never had been, though. She'd been distant at best, hostile at worst. Thanos had always had it made clear to him that he was a spare and useless prince around the court, and a lot of that had been Athena's doing.

"I was trying to protect my son," she said. "You went after him, didn't you? Did you find him in Felldust?"

"I did," Thanos admitted, and in that one brief moment, he did feel sorry for her. It had to be a hard thing hearing that your son was dead.

She sat there, and didn't even try to hold back the tears that fell then.

"My son," she murmured. "My beautiful son."

Her beautiful son who had been a monster. Who had looked like everyone's dream of a prince and turned lives into nightmares. Thanos reached out to touch her shoulder then, and Athena pulled back. He watched her piecing her composure back together, and when she looked up at him again, there was no trace of her grief, she'd buried it that deep.

"I should hate you," she said. "But the truth is that I set this in motion. Lucious was… he was mad. Stephania is just evil. She has treated me like this. She has tricked and abused you. I want you to kill her. I want you to do that, as your penance for killing my son."

"As my penance?" Thanos echoed. He couldn't believe that she was thinking like that. "I'm here to save Ceres."

"And Stephania has her," Athena said. "Do you know all the ways into the castle? Do you know the tunnels?"

"I know some," Thanos said. "I made it inside without the guards spotting me."

He had the sense that they were bargaining now, but he didn't have enough time to bargain. Outside, he could still hear the sounds of the battle raging, the screams of men and women as they were dragged out into the streets.

"And you think that's what you need to do now?" Athena countered. "Look around you. *Look*. The city has fallen. The castle *will* fall. And when it does… I can guess which of the tunnels Stephania will take, where it will come out. She'll run, and you can be there when she does."

"I'm not here for Stephania," Thanos said, although he couldn't help thinking about her then. He'd gone there before to try to get her out, and she still mattered. It was just… this was about Ceres. Wasn't it?

"Do you think they won't be together?" Athena said. "Do you think she won't keep Ceres with her? She was planning to use her to bargain. Besides, those two are bound together as long as they both love you. They'll keep coming back together. It's inevitable."

Thanos hoped that wasn't true. He really hoped that he and Ceres and Stephania wouldn't be caught up like that for the rest of their lives. He could believe Athena's reasoning though. Stephania would sit safe until she thought there was nothing to do but run, and then she would abandon everything.

And yes, she might take Ceres with her.

"How about if I sweeten this?" Athena said. "I know where you can find out more about your mother."

"In Felldust," Thanos said. "I know."

"Is that what Claudius told you?" Athena countered. She smiled. "My husband had many fine qualities, but he wasn't good at keeping track of things. *I* kept my eyes on your mother, because I don't like having rivals too close at hand. My people almost took her in Felldust. It was probably why she moved on."

Thanos stared at her. Only Athena would admit that she was planning to kill someone's mother, right to their face. But then, he had just admitted what he'd done to Lucious, hadn't he?

"Where?" Thanos asked.

"Promise that you'll kill Stephania, give me a way out of here, and I'll tell you."

Thanos swallowed. He wanted to know, but there was only so much he could promise.

"I'm going after Ceres," he said. "If I run into Stephania I'll… I'll do whatever I think is right. As for getting you out of here, there are small boats on the shore, and people I brought are creating a distraction even now. I can't give you more than that."

Athena sat there, seeming to consider it. She actually sat there as though this were some negotiation she could just walk away from. Finally, she stood.

"Very well," she said. "There is a spot nearby, among three cedar trees, behind a statue of the masked revelers. That is the escape route I would use if I were Stephania. As for your mother, she fled to the lands of the cloud palaces."

That was far enough that Thanos winced at the thought of having to travel there. The lands were notoriously difficult to travel through, with their warring clans and their mountainous islands.

"I've done my part," Athena said. She stood. "For what it's worth, I wish that things could have been different between us."

"So do I," Thanos said, but Athena was already gone, slipping off toward the water.

CHAPTER TWENTY FIVE

Ceres sprinted after Stephania, following the tunnels even though she could barely see now without her brother's torch. The need to see Stephania punished for everything she'd done drove her on. She wasn't going to get away from this without cost, the way she seemed to have gotten away with so much else in her life.

Ceres could feel the weight of the swords in her hands. Stephania had killed so many people. She'd murdered them to keep secrets and to hurt Ceres, to grab power and to try to hang on to it. By any standard, she deserved death.

Ceres saw sunlight ahead and ran toward it. If Stephania got out into the open air, there would be too many directions she could go in. Ceres might be able to move faster than her, but she wouldn't be able to find her.

She broke out into the open air and found herself in a spot that seemed incongruous in the middle of Delos. Statues surrounded the entrance, representing gods and goddesses so old Ceres couldn't begin to name them, half of them worn smooth with time. A few trees enclosed a green space, with a fountain at the center. It was the kind of place that might have been planned and then forgotten about, left as a way to disguise the tunnel entrance, or that might have grown up by accident.

Stephania was there, but not in the way Ceres expected. She was currently face down in the fountain, kicking and struggling as another figure held her there. The woman wore strips of cloth wound round her in the fashion of Felldust, and if it had been anyone but Stephania, Ceres would have rushed forward to help. Then there was what she was saying.

"And this is for everything you did to Thanos. He saved me, and you treated him like he was..." She looked up, obviously hearing Ceres approach. She hauled Stephania up, wrenching her arm behind her back in a way that made her wince.

Good. As far as Ceres was concerned, she deserved that, and more than that. Even so, Ceres kept her hands on her swords.

"Who are you?" Ceres asked. "What are you doing here? How do you know Thanos?"

Ceres saw the other woman look her up and down. "Stephania? Who is *this*?"

Ceres heard Stephania laugh at that, the sound coming out as a series of spluttering coughs.

"Do you hear that, Ceres? You're unrecognizable now. Thanks to—"

The other woman cut her off by dunking her head back under the water.

"Ceres? You're Ceres?" Again, Ceres saw the other woman looking her over. She flashed a smile, sudden and bright. "Yes, I can see what he sees in you. If I weren't dying…"

She pulled Stephania up, gasping.

"Who are you?" Ceres asked again. "What are you doing here?"

"My name is Felene," she replied. "My story is a long and complex one, and the bards had better learn to sing it right when I'm gone. Felene, the pirate who tracked a princess across continents for revenge. There's a song in that, don't you think?"

Frankly, Ceres suspected that she might be drunk. Even so, right then, anyone who had Stephania's arm twisted painfully behind her back probably counted as a friend.

"Forgive me if I ramble," Felene said. "But *someone* stabbed me in the back over in Felldust, and the delirium is getting a bit"—she broke into a fit of coughing—"much. Now where was I? *This* is for making me kill a woman who had the most gorgeous eyes I've ever seen."

She dunked Stephania back under the water of the fountain. To her own surprise, Ceres found herself stepping forward, reaching out an arm to pull Felene back. The look she gave Ceres as Stephania came up gasping had hard edges, but also a hint of confusion to it.

"There was a time I'd have punched you for putting your hands on me like that," Felene said. She winced. "Which probably says something unfortunate about my life. What? Do you want to take a turn drowning her?"

Ceres shook her head. "This is cruel, Felene. I don't know you, but I know Thanos, and he wouldn't travel with someone who would torture someone to death."

She saw Felene's expression soften a little. She flung Stephania down at Ceres's feet so suddenly that Ceres had to take a step back.

"Thanos is the soft-hearted one," Felene said. "I'm frankly astonished he's lived this long. Still, you're right. If you want someone dead, you kill them. No amount of pain is going to undo what she's done."

Ceres could understand the desire to hurt Stephania. It was there inside her too. A part of her wanted to beat Stephania. To cut her in retaliation for everything that Stephania had done to her.

Ceres wasn't going to do that, though. Not because she didn't think Stephania deserved it, but because *she* didn't deserve to have to do it.

"You *are* going to kill her though?" Felene asked. "If you don't want to do it, I will, but… I figure she's hurt you more than anyone. More even than me, and she's *killed* me."

Ceres nodded. She put away one of her blades, grabbing Stephania's hair so that she could bare her throat. Stephania stared up at Ceres, and Ceres could see the fear there, but she could also see the defiance.

"So you're just going to cut my throat in cold blood?" Stephania demanded.

"I'm going to execute you for all the crimes you've committed," Ceres countered.

Stephania twisted in her grip, managing to get to her feet. This would have been so much easier if Ceres had still had the powers of her Ancient One blood. Stephania would already have been stone.

"My crimes?" Stephania said. "What about *your* crimes? You overthrew the Empire that brought stability to this region. You butchered its troops and plotted to bring down its king. Why?"

"So that people could be free," Ceres replied. She wasn't going to let Stephania pretend that they were somehow the same.

"And are they?" Stephania asked. She gestured, as if to take in the city. "You took away the only thing holding back invaders from outside. The people of this city will be slaves, or slaughtered. All their deaths are on *your* conscience."

The hard part of that was that it was true. If Ceres and the rebellion hadn't risen up, the Empire would still be exactly what it had always been. It would be filled with crushing inequalities, run by rapacious nobles, and take everything from the poorest, but it wouldn't be *this*.

"This came out of the war for it," Ceres said. "Not out of what we were trying to do."

"And did you think there wouldn't be a war?" Stephania demanded. "Are you that naïve that you thought the Empire would just hand over its power?"

Ceres couldn't believe this. Was Stephania trying to tell her that all this was her fault for trying to change things and make them better?

Stephania wasn't done either, it seemed.

"Let me tell you how things could have been," she said. "If you hadn't shown up, I would have married Thanos without any of the things that happened later. I would have maneuvered for power in the Empire for both of us, and we would have gotten it."

"You in power?" Felene said from the side. "Are we supposed to pretend that's a good thing?"

Ceres could see that she was getting restless. She had a knife in her hand now, and was shifting her grip on it as she waited.

"Me and Thanos in power," Stephania replied. "Do you think we wouldn't make good rulers? His sense of fairness. My understanding of what it takes to rule. I am not cruel for the sake of it. I could have been a great queen, beside Thanos."

The hardest part was that it was probably true. Ceres knew enough about Stephania to know that she could be kind to those around her as well as cruel. She thought of herself first, but she wasn't Lucious.

Ceres could see how it might have happened. Lucious would have had some kind of accident. News about Thanos's birth would have been spread as rumors. Eventually, Claudius would have adopted him formally as his heir. Perhaps Stephania was right. Perhaps she and Thanos would have been the perfect ruling couple. Perhaps it would have been some great time for the Empire, achieving more for its people than invasion and death.

None of that mattered though.

"I don't care," Ceres said. "You had me tortured. You were going to kill me. You *have* killed people who followed me, who were my friends."

"And you've killed how many imperial guards?" Stephania demanded. "How many of my handmaidens are dead or in the hands of Felldust's warriors thanks to you?"

Ceres didn't know. She wasn't even sure that she could explain the difference, except by saying that they'd chosen that fight, and that she'd tried to save lives where she could.

"Is it just that they're not on your side?" Stephania asked. "You've decided you're good, so anything you do must be good? Invading a city? Killing the nobles there? How many people have you turned to stone? How many are worse off now, because of—"

"Enough talking," Felene snapped. "We aren't here for a philosophy lesson. If you want a reason to do it, my murder is more than enough. Kill her."

Ceres knew that Felene was right. This was the moment when it had to happen. She couldn't leave Stephania alive behind her; not when it meant that she would just keep coming after her. Leave her alive, and Ceres would never be safe.

She lifted her blade, ready to thrust it into Stephania's heart. Unlike her, Ceres wasn't going to drag this out. *That* was one difference between them. Ceres didn't want Stephania to suffer. She just wanted this to end.

Stephania seemed to sense what was going to happen, because she backed away until she was pressed against one of the statues there. She looked around as if seeking somewhere to run, but there was nowhere for her to go.

Ceres readied herself, determined to strike true.

CHAPTER TWENTY SIX

Thanos ran for the spot Athena had told him about, trying to recall her directions as he hurried through the streets.

"The spot with the statues and trees," Thanos said to himself. In Delos, there were plenty of spots like that, where greenery intruded on the marble and stone of the city's buildings. There were fewer of them in the poorer districts, though. Nobles didn't see the point in providing them for ordinary people.

He tried to make sense of the streets around him, recalling all he could about the city's layout. He'd been out into the city more than most nobles, but even so, finding his way was far from easy. Especially not when there were invaders there.

Thanos pressed himself back into a doorway, trying to stay quiet, as a group moved past.

Which way from here? He wished he'd thought to make the queen come with him and show him, but there would have been dangers in doing that too. She might not have been able to keep to the shadows as easily. She certainly wouldn't have been able to do what Thanos did next, which was climb onto one of the nearby roofs, looking for a spot that matched her description.

He saw a space not far away that had trees around it and a fountain in the middle. When he saw what was happening there, Thanos skidded down from the roof, landing hard and redoubling his efforts. He hoped that he would be in time.

"Ceres! Wait!"

He didn't dare call out too loud, in case he brought down trouble on all of them. Yet he had to risk *something*, because if he didn't…

He reached the circle at a full run, sprinting in between two of the statues. Ceres stood with Stephania pinned back against a statue, her sword drawn back ready to strike her through the heart. But to Thanos, it looked as though she was about to thrust the blade through Stephania's stomach, slaying her and her child together.

"Stop!" Thanos yelled, running into the circle of grass and trees.

Ceres was there, and Stephania, and, incredibly, Felene. Thanos had never thought that he would see the three of them in the same place together.

"What's going on here?" he demanded.

To his surprise, Felene stepped in front of him, as if to hold him back. "An execution. One that's long overdue."

Thanos shook his head. "I can't let that happen. Ceres, this is wrong."

He started to move past her, but she moved back into the way. Ceres looked around, and he could see the hurt there.

"You want to stop me killing *her*?" Ceres demanded.

"I want to stop you from killing her *child*," he corrected.

She seemed to soften a bit at that.

Then her look hardened.

"Not to mention your wife," Stephania spat from her spot by the statue.

Thanos saw Ceres tense, and he pushed past Felene, grabbing for her arm. His fingers closed around it, and a part of him still expected to be flung back by the powers within her even though he'd heard about Stephania poisoning her. He expected Ceres to rip free, but for once, Thanos was stronger.

She looked back at him, and she just looked hurt then.

"She's killed so many people, Thanos," Ceres said. "And you just want to forgive her?"

Felene chipped in at that point. "She doesn't get to walk away from this free, Thanos. She tricked me, and then stabbed me in the back. I... I'm dying because of her."

Thanos stared at her. He'd only known Felene for a brief time, but that news was like a punch to the stomach. He could see why Felene would want Stephania dead. He could see why anyone would. After all, he'd killed Lucious for only a little more. Thanos shook his head. He knew that there were some things that couldn't be forgiven. That wasn't the point.

"I'm not looking to forgive anything," he said. "But Stephania is pregnant with my child. It broke something in me when I thought I'd lost that because of Lucious. It would be worse losing it because of you. Lucious was a monster, and you're anything but that."

Still, Ceres hesitated.

"When you left, I was worried that you kept going back to her," she said. "I was worried because you chose to marry her, settle down with her, have a child with her. You keep saying that it isn't Stephania you want—but you don't act like it."

Thanos could understand that. It seemed sometimes that the world was conspiring to push him and Stephania together. Yet the truth was that it wasn't her he loved.

"Please," he said. "This isn't about her. It's about us. If you do this, then every time I look at you, I'll find myself wondering about what my child might have grown up to be. I'd find myself hating you, and I can't imagine myself hating you, Ceres."

She paused for a moment, and Thanos could see her arguing with herself. She still held the sword tightly, and Thanos didn't know what he would do if she thrust the blade at Stephania.

Would he be able to act in time if she did? Would he be able to get between her and Stephania? Would he fight Ceres to save Stephania? Fight the woman he loved to save the mother of his child? Could he bring himself to do that?

He didn't need to answer that question though, because finally, mercifully, Ceres stepped back.

"Are you sure that this isn't about what you feel, Thanos?" Ceres demanded.

Stephania chose that moment to speak, stepping away from the statue and moving around to where Ceres couldn't just thrust a blade into her. Thanos really wished that she hadn't.

"We could still be good together, Thanos. I know you still feel *something*, even if you want to pretend that you don't."

Thanos stood there, unable to speak. Did Stephania really think that things could still work out between the two of them?

"You came back to save me," Stephania said. "You sent Felene to carry me across the sea to safety. A man who feels nothing wouldn't do that."

"*I* wish you hadn't," Felene said with a wince. She leaned against the nearest statue, coughing. The back of her hand was wet with blood when she was finished. "I'm really starting to wish I hadn't stopped drowning her."

Thanos could understand that, and guilt flashed through him at having brought the thief to this.

"There's still a way out of this," Stephania said.

"Yes," Ceres said. "We run."

Thanos saw Stephania shake her head in disagreement. "This isn't about *you*. It's about us. Thanos, and me."

Thanos held up a hand to stop her. "This isn't about us, Stephania."

All this time, and she still wasn't prepared to accept it.

"We're still married," Stephania said. "We're still having this child. And we can have *so* much more. We can still come out of this situation ahead."

Thanos heard Felene snort.

"Honestly, what did you ever see in her?" she demanded. "Days at sea with her, and all she did was whine. And now this nonsense. Just clap a hand over her mouth so that we can go without attracting the attention of every warrior in the city."

That was a real concern. Thanos had seen what was happening in the city. His small boat would still be there, and if he was lucky, they might be able to catch up with the smuggling boat to go further, but they needed to move *now*. Hesitate much longer, and they would lose their route out of there, right at the moment when soldiers would be coming for them.

"Felene is right," Ceres said. "We need to go. I don't know how many soldiers will have followed us down the tunnels beneath the city."

"And there are plenty around on the streets," Felene said.

To Thanos's surprise, Stephania didn't seem put off by that.

"Then we bring them to us," she said.

Thanos frowned at that. "What?"

He was more convinced than ever that she wasn't thinking clearly, although the truth was that Stephania had always been good at hiding what she thought from him. She'd plotted behind his back for almost as long as he'd known her, and Thanos had only known about what she was doing for a short time.

"I had to run when they broke into the castle," Stephania said. She glared at Ceres. "You ruined that plan, but there are still ways back."

"Stephania—" Thanos began.

"The warriors of Felldust value strength and cunning," Stephania insisted. "A leader is only a leader for as long as he can hold onto his power. Between us, you and I have all the cunning and strength we could need."

Thanos couldn't quite believe what he was hearing. Even so, he felt as though he ought to check.

"You want to challenge the First Stone?" he asked.

"I want *you* to challenge him," Stephania said. "I can get us to him. I can convince him to fight. You can kill him, and I will be able to turn that into more, by persuading them that it means you have succeeded him. We couldn't stop the invasion, but we could control it so it hurt far fewer people."

Thanos heard Ceres scoff at that.

"So it didn't hurt *you*, you mean?" she said. "If it were that simple, why couldn't I just walk up and kill him?"

"Because this isn't just about cutting the head from the snake," Stephania snapped back. "You're thinking like some kind of bard's song, where the hero walks up and kills their foe and that's it."

Thanos found himself cocking his head to one side. "Isn't that what you're proposing I do?"

Stephania shook her head. "It's more than that. It's politics. It's not enough to kill him. You have to look as though you can succeed him. *She* couldn't do that, but *we* could. The current queen of the Empire and her husband, joining with Felldust not by being conquered, but by taking a position within it. It's a story they could believe. A story they could get behind."

Thanos couldn't believe that she was actually suggesting this. She made it sound so easy, as if they could just walk up and steal someone else's invasion from them. Then again, it was what she'd done with the throne of the Empire, wasn't it?

"You're mad," Felene said. "A country isn't just some bauble that you can lift from a rich man's corpse."

"How else do you think people get them?" Stephania demanded. She looked back to Thanos. "We can do this, Thanos, and it would be good for the Empire. Felldust is going to finish its invasion, but together, we could control how it happens. We could limit the damage. And our child would be heir to the whole of Felldust, as well as the Empire. We could do this."

Thanos could hear the determination there, and for a moment he could feel himself being carried along by it. Perhaps it would be possible to do it. Perhaps he could just take over Irrien's seat, and stop the worst excesses of the invasion. If he could save people like that, didn't he have a duty to do it?

Then he looked across at Ceres, and knew that he could never really do it. Stephania's answer meant staying with her. It meant trusting her and working alongside her. Thanos couldn't do any of those things. Especially not when Stephania would probably use any power she got as a way to strike out at Ceres.

"No," Thanos said. "No, I'm not going to do it. I know you, Stephania. Even if by some miracle all this worked, you'd be plotting the moment we got into any kind of power. Tell me that you wouldn't try to kill Ceres the moment you had the opportunity."

"We could let her live if that's what you wanted," Stephania said.

Thanos looked over at her, then at Ceres, then back again. The truth was that it wasn't even a choice, not anymore. Whatever he'd once had with Stephania, it wasn't the same as the things he felt for Ceres. Stephania had tried to paint a picture of the two of them living together in harmony, but the truth was that the only one of them Thanos could picture himself with was Ceres.

"No," he said. "*This* is what is going to happen. We're going to get out of here, all of us. You're going to live, because you're carrying my child, but when that child is born, you'll go, and we'll never see you again. I won't be caught up in your plots, Stephania. It isn't you I want. It is Ceres."

Stephania scowled.

"You think you get to decide what happens to me?" Stephania demanded. "You think you get to choose for me?"

She took a breath, and Thanos guessed what she was going to do a moment before she did it. But he wasn't fast enough to move in and stop her.

She shouted, loud enough that no one in the docks could have helped but hear it.

"Warriors of Felldust! We're over here!"

She looked back at Thanos in something like triumph.

"It looks as though we'll have to go with my plan after all, doesn't it?"

CHAPTER TWENTY SEVEN

Stephania smiled in triumph as the others looked at her in shock. Did they really think that they got to decide what happened to her? Did they think that they could just condemn her to a life where her child would be taken from her? When she would be cast aside to be less than nothing?

She would fight off the world rather than let that happen. No one would take what was hers. Not Felldust's sorcerers, not the nobles of Delos, and certainly not Thanos. She would die before she let that happen.

She would kill before she let that happen.

"What have you done, you arrogant idiot?" Felene demanded.

Stephania's smile tightened, tempered only by the knowledge that the thief was dying. As she should have back on Felldust. If she'd had the grace to do that, Stephania would already have been away from there.

"She's done what she always does," Ceres said. "Acted with as much bile as she can because she isn't getting her own way."

She made it sound as though Stephania was a child, rather than a newly crowned queen.

Even Thanos seemed shocked by the move. That was Ceres's fault, no doubt. If he'd been there alone, Stephania would have been able to persuade him. They'd have been killing the First Stone even then.

"Stephania, how could you do this?" Thanos asked.

Stephania had done it for the same reason she did everything else: because it was necessary. Now there was no way out but through this.

"They'll be coming," Stephania said to him. "Stay here. Fight them. Help me to kill their leader. We can do this, Thanos. We can save Delos. We can *rule* it."

She could rule it. Stephania had felt what it meant to be a ruler. She wasn't going to give that up, and if it meant that she got Thanos too—

Felene cut her off with a slap that rocked her. "We need to get out of here," she said to the others, as if Stephania were just a distraction. When she turned to Stephania, Stephania could see the hatred there. "Run if you want to live. Just don't pick the same direction as us, or I'll cut your throat, child or no child."

"No," Thanos said. "We take her with us. I'll bind and drag her if I have to. Just until the child is born. Please."

Stephania saw Ceres nod, although she could see that the peasant wasn't happy about it.

"All right," Ceres said. "You get her arms, I'll—"

Stephania reacted on instinct, her hand diving into the folds of her dress for one of the daggers she kept there. She didn't have many weapons left, but she would use every one she had to keep them from taking her child. She would not be treated as no more than the vessel to bear Thanos's baby. The sorcerer had tried to do that, and now her husband was… no, she wouldn't allow it!

She leapt forward, springing past Felene, a blade in her hand as she sprang for Thanos and Ceres.

She hadn't reckoned how fast Felene was, even injured.

Felene sprang in the way as quick as a snake, and Stephania felt her blade, meant for Thanos, sink deep into the other woman's chest. Of course, *this* time it would be that easy. If she'd managed it so cleanly back on the boat, maybe they wouldn't be standing there now.

Felene's face was set with determination as she punched Stephania back, knocking her sprawling.

Ceres went one better, kicking the knife out of Stephania's hand.

Stephania ran for the edge of the circle of statues, but Ceres was faster. So was Thanos. Stephania felt their hands close on her arms, pulling her back even though she fought.

"If you don't kill her now—" Ceres began.

"What?" Stephania demanded. "What will you do? Leave him? You care so little for him, don't you?"

She did it because she could. Because even driving that small wedge between Ceres and Thanos was something. Stephania saw the look that passed between Ceres and Thanos. She saw the look of confusion and hurt on Thanos's face as he fought to work out what to do next. She enjoyed that. She couldn't have him, but at least she could make sure that Ceres didn't get him.

"I… I still can't kill her," Thanos said.

"I can," Ceres replied.

Stephania saw Thanos pull at her arm. She smiled at that.

"Oh, how sweet," Stephania said. "The noble prince, protecting his wife. His *wife*, Ceres."

She didn't care how angry she made Ceres then. Angry was good. Angry meant that she wouldn't be thinking. Stephania might get another chance to strike.

"What do you want, Thanos?" Ceres asked. "We *can't* take her with us. She'd kill us at the first opportunity she got."

"Yes, Thanos," Stephania asked, as sweetly as she could, "what do you want? What do you *really* want?"

Sometimes, the only weapons she had were words, but Stephania was an expert when it came to using them.

"I can't kill her," Thanos said. "And I can't let you kill her, Ceres, because I wouldn't be able to look at you the same way again."

"Thanos—" Ceres began, and Stephania smiled in victory.

"But I can leave her behind," Thanos suddenly said. His hands tightened on Stephania's arms, catching her as she realized what he'd just said. "I can leave her to the fate of Felldust's army."

Stephania felt a wave of terror overcome her.

"No," Stephania begged. "They'll kill me. They'll do *worse* than kill me. Please, Thanos."

He didn't answer, though, but instead dragged her in the direction of one of the nearest statues.

"You can't leave me here to die!" she shrieked. "To be raped! To be tortured! To be made a mockery of!"

Yet she saw Thanos's expression and her terror increased as she knew her pleas were falling on deaf ears.

"I'll kill you," Stephania shrieked, filled with rage, desperate. "I'll kill you both!"

Thanos wrenched her arms behind her back, while Ceres cut away Stephania's belt and then tied her arms in place. Stephania wrenched at the bonds, trying to pull her arms free, but nothing happened.

Worse, she saw Felene struggling to her feet, drawing a sword and long knife.

"Go..." the sailor managed. "I'll hold them off."

"Felene," Ceres began.

"*Go!*"

Stephania could not believe it as she watched Thanos and Ceres run off, leaving her like this. She vowed her hatred with every step they took.

"Looks like it's just you and me, princess," Felene said. "Don't worry... I'm not... going to kill you. You deserve... far worse than that."

Stephania ignored her and kept working at her bonds, trying to break free, trying to get away before...

They came in a rush, the first men of Felldust bursting into the circle of grass while Felene moved forward to face them. Stephania saw her thrust a blade through one warrior's chest, parry a blow from a second, and cut across the throat of a third.

She wasn't moving well, though. Stephania had seen how fast she could be when she'd fought Elethe, but now she staggered from blow to blow.

Good.

Stephania watched as a warrior thrust a spear into the thief. Felene cut back, bringing the warrior down, but another cut across her leg. She collapsed, and the warriors stepped back the way they might have from a wounded omnicat.

Stephania recognized First Stone Irrien as he stepped into the circle formed by the trees. He was everything her spies had said: tall, imposing, cruelly handsome and deadly looking. Felene fell to her side as he approached, hefting an axe with one hand.

"You're the First Stone?" she demanded.

He nodded to her. "I am."

She forced a smile. "Good, I've… been waiting for someone… worthy of killing me."

"Then I'm sorry I didn't get here earlier," he said. "Rest now. Your part in this is done."

Felene lay there, coughing up blood, as he walked past her as if she weren't there.

And then, to Stephania's horror, she spoke her final words:

"And that is Stephania," Felene said. "Don't let her…tell you otherwise."

Felene then collapsed, dead.

Stephania felt a rush of fear as the ruler of Felldust grinned in surprise and delight. Felene had ruined her one chance to pretend she was someone else. In her dying breath, Felene had somehow managed to kill her.

He stalked toward her and lifted his axe. For a moment, Stephania thought that he might cut her down, and she flinched back against the statue, unable to stop her fear.

He buried the axe in the ground, then reached out a hand to touch her face. Stephania wanted to pull away, but she wouldn't show that weakness. She *wouldn't*.

"Lady Stephania," he said. "Tales of your beauty do not do you justice."

There was still a chance. The First Stone was still a man, still a ruler, still a warrior. All three of those were things Stephania could work with. She could come out of this more powerful than she'd gone into it.

"First Stone Irrien," she said. "Welcome to Delos. I hope you're enjoying your time here."

She tried to make it sound as if they were meeting in the middle of some noble masque, not the aftermath of an invasion. Pretend a thing enough, she'd always found, and the reality would follow.

"Someone certainly seems to have left me the most interesting things."

He reached out to touch her throat this time. Stephania tried not to think about how easily he could crush that throat.

"I hope I will prove more interesting than you think," Stephania said. "If you know who I am, you know what I can do for you."

"You sound as if you are proposing an alliance," Irrien said. He sounded amused by it, but also interested.

Stephania knew that she had him then. She might be the one tied in place, but soon enough, Irrien would be the one with her strings around him. She would have to be careful at first, have to suggest and persuade rather than demand, but she could do this.

"I am currently the most important noble of the Empire," Stephania said. "I took its throne by force and cunning." The two things that they admired most in Felldust. "While you are a man without a wife."

"You're proposing marriage?" Irrien asked, moving behind Stephania, slicing through her bonds with a knife. "You're bold indeed."

She resisted the urge to rub her wrists. That would have looked weak. Instead, she stood before him the way a ruler should.

"The strong are bold," Stephania said. "And we could do great things together. I know the Empire, all its secrets, all its webs of connections. More than that, I bring a sense of legitimacy. We could join our lands together formally, ruling both, above my nobles and your fellow stones."

"It is a tempting offer," Irrien admitted.

She could tempt him more than that. She moved close, pressing against him.

"And if your walls had held," Irrien went on, "I might have considered it. Now, though, you have nothing to give I cannot take."

"What?"

Stephania moved to step back, but Irrien caught her by the throat, sudden and tight. She grabbed for his hand, but couldn't move it. His other hand moved to her dress, and Stephania cried out as he ripped the outer layers from her.

He threw her to the ground, and Stephania lay there, staring up at him in terror. When he reached to his belt and drew out a whip, she shrank back.

"Do not worry though. I won't be killing you. You will make far too fine a slave for that."

Stephania wanted to stand, to argue, to fight, but there was no time to do any of it. The first blow struck her, and all she could do was scream.

CHAPTER TWENTY EIGHT

Ceres leaned on Thanos as much as he leaned on her as they made their way down toward the docks. Thanks to everything she'd suffered, she felt as though she barely had the strength to stand, while he seemed to be unwilling to risk letting go of her, even for a moment.

"That way," Thanos managed, pointing. "There are small boats."

Ceres nodded, trying to steer the two of them in the direction he'd pointed. She tried to keep to the shadows to keep them from being spotted, but the truth was that they needed to move quickly more than they needed to keep out of sight.

Somewhere behind them, Ceres heard Stephania scream, and she felt Thanos tense. For a moment, she found herself wondering if he would run back for her. He'd done it before, hadn't he? He'd returned to Delos to save her.

He pressed forward, though, and Ceres dared to breathe a sigh of relief. Maybe they could do this. Maybe they could get through it.

Ceres saw a group of Felldust warriors ahead, looting their way along one of the streets. There couldn't be much in the way of pickings for them by now, but they seemed to be going through the houses anyway, determined to collect every scrap they could.

Ceres pulled Thanos down a side street, looking to dodge past them. She hurried with him, making her way past a water butt, then over a low fence. They paused for a moment, waiting for more soldiers to pass. In that moment, Thanos said the words that Ceres both wanted to hear and dreaded.

"I love you," he said.

"I love you too, Thanos," Ceres said. "But can't this wait until we're clear?"

She wanted to put this off if she could. Thanos had gone with her. He'd rejected Stephania, but even so, there were so many things they needed to talk about.

"No," Thanos said. "I mean it. I mean… I love you, not Stephania. I chose you. I *choose* you."

That was good to hear, but it was something Thanos had said before. He'd still gone back for Stephania, hadn't he? He'd still kept Ceres from killing her. Ceres understood that was about Stephania being the mother of his child, but that didn't make it better. It meant that there would always be something connecting Thanos and Stephania together.

On the other hand, he had left her. He'd tied her there for Felldust's warriors. Maybe that was as clear a choice as Ceres was going to get.

That was a question for later, though. For now, the only thing they could do was try to get out of the city alive.

Ceres kept picking twists and turns through the city, trying to dodge the soldiers there. She knew the streets, thanks to all the times she'd delivered weapons for her father or picked up food from the markets. She wove her way through the small streets and alleyways, trying to find a route that Felldust's soldiers wouldn't block.

She didn't succeed.

Three soldiers came out of a house just as they passed, and Ceres's breath caught. They stood there for a moment, staring at the two of them as though not able to understand who they were.

Ceres was tired, but she still had enough energy left to react first. She drew a sword with her off hand, thrusting it up under the breastplate of one of the invaders as she drew her second.

Thanos stepped past her, parrying a strike aimed at her head. The attacker pushed him back into Ceres, but Ceres saw him thrust around the attacker's guard, deep under his collarbone. Ceres rode the motion, striking for the last enemy. Off balance as she was, though, the blow fell short.

The man yelled something in the language of Felldust, and Ceres guessed that he was calling out their presence to anyone who was listening. She thrust her blade into him at the second attempt, and Thanos thrust with her, but by then, the damage was done.

"Can you go faster?" Ceres asked.

Thanos nodded. "As fast as you need to go."

Ceres didn't reply, but instead tried to rush into motion. She was bone tired, almost staggering, but she still forced herself across a flat roof, then down across the cobbles beyond.

Ceres heard someone call out behind them and risked a glance back. She saw figures in the mish-mash of different uniforms the invaders favored, rushing after them while some pointed.

"Run!" she yelled to Thanos.

He ran with her, keeping going in her wake, following her lead. They skimmed over the cobbles, heading down in the direction of the docks, moving as quickly as they could. Ceres wasn't sure that they were moving quick enough. She heard footsteps behind her, spun, and saw a spear heading for her face. She swept it aside and sent the attacker sprawling, kicking him as she went past. She saw Thanos shove aside a second attacker, throwing him into the nearest wall with sheer momentum.

Ceres kept moving, not daring to stop and fight. Every moment they spent fighting was a moment when more enemies might arrive. Soon, they would find themselves overwhelmed. It was better to run.

But running might not be enough. Even if there were boats down on the waterfront, it would still take time to get one of them into the water, to cast off, to break free. How could they do all that if there were soldiers coming after them?

They were going to die, but Ceres wasn't going to give up. She and Thanos kept going, continuing to hope.

She saw the beach ahead and pressed on as fast as she could. What she saw there lent her strength, and quickly she felt the shingle of it under her feet. There was a boat out there in the shallows and on it, Ceres could see her brother, her father, Leyana, and the combatlords Ceres had helped. They pointed as they saw her, then waved as if to make certain that she knew which way to go.

"Not far now," Ceres said. "That—"

Sand caught under her feet, and she stumbled.

She rolled back to her feet, but Thanos was already there, standing ready to meet their foes. The first to reach them died, Thanos's blade finding a home in his chest and then springing free again.

Ceres jumped past, parrying a blow from a longsword, then ducked under the sweep of a curved knife. She didn't give ground, *couldn't* give ground, because to do so would have been to leave Thanos alone to their blades. They could survive this only as long as they stood together.

She stood there and fought, chopping and parrying, feeling a sword slice a line across her abdomen because she couldn't spring aside. She heard Thanos grunt as a blade cut him, then saw him take an enemy's head from his shoulders.

Figures burst past her. The three combatlords slammed into the chasing troops, cutting down those closest and pushing back the others. Ceres glanced round to see her father standing side by side with Thanos.

"To the boat!" he yelled, and Ceres nodded.

She ran with the others into the shallows, feeling the water lap around her ankles. She thought she saw a body there, washed up from the battle, a sword still stuck through it. She was about to run past when his eyes opened, and Ceres recognized him almost in the same instant.

"Akila?"

She heard him groan. His injury looked terrible right then. How long had he been there? Ceres ran to him, ignoring the calls of the others and the threat of the soldiers approaching behind them. She knelt by Akila at the point where the tide met the shore, but she knew there was no time to be gentle about this.

"I'm sorry," she said, as she wrapped both hands around the hilt of the sword and pulled.

There was a good chance that this would kill him. Ceres had seen enough wounds to know that sometimes a blade or an arrow could be the only thing plugging a gap, staunching the blood that would otherwise flow out. But she couldn't hope to carry Akila back to the boat with the blade still in him, and it would definitely shift and cut deeper if she tried to drag him.

Akila screamed as Ceres pulled the blade out, and his screams were worse as the salt water washed over him. That was probably a good thing, though, because she'd heard of sailors washing wounds out with sea salt, and it being almost as good as cauterizing for keeping out infections.

She saw the combatlords fighting their way back to her, the soldiers of Felldust following. Ceres stepped forward as they approach, hefting the blade she'd pulled from Akila with two hands.

To her shock, the invaders stopped, staring at her. No, not at her, at the sword. Did they recognize it? They were certainly staring at it as if it were something special. Ceres couldn't understand much of what they were saying, but she thought she recognized the word "Irrien" and the word for sword.

"Irrien's sword?" she called out to them, holding it up. "Well, tell him that I'll give it back to him some time. Tell him that this isn't over."

Ceres held it between her and them, ready to strike at the first to approach. It was so heavy that it took all her strength to wield it, but it would be more than enough to smash through the guard of the first to attack.

One did, charging. Ceres ducked under his blow, then spun and cut. The sword's weight took it through his neck as if it wasn't there, slicing his head from his body as cleanly as an executioner's axe might have. Another ran in and Ceres cut across his abdomen.

Thanos was there then, lifting Akila as easily as a child. He kept behind Ceres, trusting in her skills to keep them all safe. That said more than anything about what he felt for her.

Ceres could see the combatlords moving with him, dragging Akila onto the boat, and she started to back toward it. Once again, she felt the water around her ankles. The rest of the soldiers seemed to be hanging back, none willing to be the next to die.

She felt the wood of the boat bump against her back, and passed up the sword. She wasn't going to let it go, if only because of the symbolic value that came from having it. Her father took the blade from her, and Ceres clambered up into the boat. She barely had the strength to do it. In fact, without Sartes's and Leyana's helping hands, Ceres doubted that she'd have made it in at all. It was crowded in the small boat, but there was just about enough room for all of them. It would get them away from the city, at least.

"We're in!" her father called. "Let's go!"

Someone put up the sail, and someone else grabbed oars. Ceres was too exhausted to do either. For the first time in days, she wasn't being tortured, or made to fight, or having to try to endure the worst conditions the city had. She didn't have the strength to stand right then, and it seemed that Thanos didn't have much strength left either. He lay in the bow of the boat, breathing heavily, so she crawled over to where Thanos lay, resting her head on his shoulder, looking back at the city as they sailed from it.

Behind them, Delos fell.

Parts of it burned, but only parts, and in a lot of ways that was worse than the alternative. It said that the invaders weren't there to raid and leave, that they weren't rushing in their depredations. They weren't sweeping through like a storm, but closing on the city like a vise, crushing the people there systematically. Ceres felt tears in her eyes at the thought of those people who'd trusted her enough to stay; people who were, even then, dying or being made into slaves.

But she couldn't do anything to help. All she could do was sail clear of the city, looking after the few people she cared about. She didn't know where they would go, or what they would do next, but Ceres hoped that wherever they went, she would be able to keep *them* safe.

Somehow, Ceres suspected that wouldn't be easy.

COMING SOON!

RULER, RIVAL, EXILE
(Of Crowns and Glory—Book 7)

"Morgan Rice has come up with what promises to be another brilliant series, immersing us in a fantasy of valor, honor, courage, magic and faith in your destiny. Morgan has managed again to produce a strong set of characters that make us cheer for them on every page….Recommended for the permanent library of all readers that love a well-written fantasy."
--Books and Movie Reviews, Roberto Mattos (regarding Rise of the Dragons)

RULER, RIVAL, EXILE is book #7 in Morgan Rice's bestselling epic fantasy series OF CROWNS AND GLORY, which begins with SLAVE, WARRIOR, QUEEN (Book #1), a free download.

With Delos in ruins, Ceres, Thanos and the others set sail for the last corner of freedom in the Empire: the isle of Haylon. There, they hope to regroup with the few freedom fighters left, fortify the island, and make a spectacular defense against the hordes of Felldust.

Ceres soon realizes that if they are to have any hope of defending the isle, she will need more than conventional skills: she will have to break the sorcerer's spell and regain the power of the Ancient Ones. And yet for this she must journey, alone, take the river of blood to the darkest cave in the realm, a place where neither life nor death exists, where she is more likely to come out dead than alive.

The First Stone Irrien, meanwhile, is determined to keep Stephania as his slave and to oppress Delos. But the other Stones of Felldust may have other plans.

RULER, RIVAL, EXILE tells an epic tale of tragic love, vengeance, betrayal, ambition, and destiny. Filled with unforgettable characters and heart-pounding action, it transports us into a world we will never forget, and makes us fall in love with fantasy all over again.

"An action packed fantasy sure to please fans of Morgan Rice's previous novels, along with fans of works such as The Inheritance Cycle by Christopher Paolini…. Fans of Young Adult Fiction will devour this latest work by Rice and beg for more."
--The Wanderer, A Literary Journal (regarding Rise of the Dragons)

Book #8 in OF CROWNS AND GLORY will be released soon!

Books by Morgan Rice

THE WAY OF STEEL
ONLY THE WORTHY (BOOK #1)

VAMPIRE, FALLEN
BEFORE DAWN (BOOK #1)

OF CROWNS AND GLORY
SLAVE, WARRIOR, QUEEN (BOOK #1)
ROGUE, PRISONER, PRINCESS (BOOK #2)
KNIGHT, HEIR, PRINCE (BOOK #3)
REBEL, PAWN, KING (BOOK #4)
SOLDIER, BROTHER SORCERER (BOOK #5)
HERO, TRAITOR, DAUGHTER (BOOK #6)
RULER, RIVAL, EXILE (BOOK #7)

KINGS AND SORCERERS
RISE OF THE DRAGONS
RISE OF THE VALIANT
THE WEIGHT OF HONOR
A FORGE OF VALOR
A REALM OF SHADOWS
NIGHT OF THE BOLD

THE SORCERER'S RING
A QUEST OF HEROES
A MARCH OF KINGS
A FATE OF DRAGONS
A CRY OF HONOR
A VOW OF GLORY
A CHARGE OF VALOR
A RITE OF SWORDS
A GRANT OF ARMS
A SKY OF SPELLS
A SEA OF SHIELDS
A REIGN OF STEEL
A LAND OF FIRE

A RULE OF QUEENS
AN OATH OF BROTHERS
A DREAM OF MORTALS
A JOUST OF KNIGHTS
THE GIFT OF BATTLE

THE SURVIVAL TRILOGY
ARENA ONE (Book #1)
ARENA TWO (Book #2)
ARENA THREE (Book #3)

the Vampire Journals
turned (book #1)
loved (book #2)
betrayed (book #3)
destined (book #4)
desired (book #5)
betrothed (book #6)
vowed (book #7)
found (book #8)
resurrected (book #9)
craved (book #10)
fated (book #11)
obsessed (book #12)

About Morgan Rice

Morgan Rice is the #1 bestselling and USA Today bestselling author of the epic fantasy series THE SORCERER'S RING, comprising seventeen books; of the #1 bestselling series THE VAMPIRE JOURNALS, comprising twelve books; of the #1 bestselling series THE SURVIVAL TRILOGY, a post-apocalyptic thriller comprising three books; of the epic fantasy series KINGS AND SORCERERS, comprising six books; and of the new epic fantasy series OF CROWNS AND GLORY. Morgan's books are available in audio and print editions, and translations are available in over 25 languages.

Morgan loves to hear from you, so please feel free to visit www.morganricebooks.com to join the email list, receive a free book, receive free giveaways, download the free app, get the latest exclusive news, connect on Facebook and Twitter, and stay in touch!

www.ingramcontent.com/pod-product-compliance
Lightning Source LLC
Chambersburg PA
CBHW070959120726
47910CB00004B/1297